Tag was no longer interested in playing nice.

He was close enough to feel the heat coming off Mia's body, to smell his soap on her skin. She moved toward him in a sweet collision. Her breasts crushed against his chest, her thighs pressed against his. All those layers of clothes couldn't keep him from remembering what she'd felt like naked in his arms.

And wanting a repeat.

Keeping his hands off her was impossible. So he slid a hand around the back of her neck, tracing the soft skin, loving how the small tendrils of hair clung to his fingers as he drew her closer. She made a small, throaty sound, tipping her head back against the door, and he was lost.

He covered her mouth with his and kissed her. He felt the strangest sense of coming home.

He wanted her, every stubborn, prickly and sensuous inch of her.

Never mind they were both leaving and he probably had no business touching her. Instead of stopping, though, he deepened their kiss.

Her lips parted beneath his, but there wasn't an ounce of submission in her. *Trap.* She lured him in in the best kind of sensual ambush, making a sound that was part delight, part moan. He threaded his fingers through her free hand, pinning it above her head. Her fingers closed around his in response, and he couldn't have broken free if he wanted to. Instead, he drank in the little sounds she made as her tongue tangled with his and they both fought to control the kiss and the heat. Kissing and kissing.

Because admitting defeat wasn't something either of them did...

Dear Reader,

I love military heroes. The men and women who serve step up and put it all on the line in situations I can't begin to imagine. Tag Johnson, the hero of *Wicked Secrets*, is a US Navy rescue swimmer. He and his teammates are the first in the water when a plane goes down in the ocean, a ship founders or a tsunami hits. The heroine of *Wicked Secrets* is also a military veteran. Mia Brandt served in the US Army and, now that she's come home, she wants to feel *normal*. Our female military veterans face an additional set of challenges when they leave active duty. From assumptions made in doctors' waiting rooms and by Veterans Affairs (that they are there as wives, mothers and girlfriends rather than as veterans themselves) to balancing motherhood and marriage with overseas deployments, they face a unique set of challenges. I loved having the chance to explore what happens when a not-quite-perfect female soldier comes home from active duty and two people wounded in different ways fall unexpectedly in love.

I hope you enjoy *Wicked Secrets*—and that you'll check out Tag's fellow rescue swimmers in *Wicked Sexy* and *Wicked Nights*. I love hearing from readers. You can find me at facebook.com/annemarshauthor or drop by my website, anne-marsh.com.

All my best,

Anne

New York Times Bestselling Author

Anne Marsh

———

Wicked Secrets

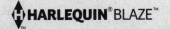

Recycling programs
for this product may
not exist in your area.

ISBN-13: 978-0-373-79843-8

Wicked Secrets

Printed in U.S.A.

www.Harlequin.com

Anne Marsh writes sexy contemporary and paranormal romances because the world can always enjoy one more alpha male. She started writing romance after getting laid off from her job as a technical writer—and quickly decided happily-ever-afters trumped software manuals. She lives in Northern California with her family and six cats.

Books by Anne Marsh

HARLEQUIN BLAZE

Wicked Sexy
Wicked Nights

To get the inside scoop on Harlequin Blaze and its talented writers, be sure to check out blazeauthors.com.

All backlist available in ebook format.

Visit the Author Profile page at Harlequin.com for more titles.

This book is for that handful of readers who go above and beyond: Rhea, Tracie, Gwen, Natalie, Brenda, Margreet, Nicola and all the other wonderful members of my street team. Your support and encouragement mean the world to me!

1

DISCOVERY ISLAND CAME with its own resident Adonis. That particular plus had definitely not been in the travel brochures Laurel, Mia Brandt's cousin and the bride-to-be, had waved enthusiastically when proposing a four day bachelorette cruise from San Francisco to Cabo San Lucas. The woman was a travel agent; she should have known the man candy would be even more of a draw than discounted cabins.

Fifty yards away from Mia's perch in the beachside bar, the hottie masterfully coaxed a boat motor to life while she stared. He might have been working in the shallow water with his back to Mia's group, but the sheer size and power of him demanded a second look, as did the effortless way he dominated his surroundings. In a firefight, she would have taken him out first, because everything about him screamed trouble.

As soon as the hostess had shown Mia to her seat, she'd spotted him at two o'clock. Cataloging her surroundings was second nature, the end result of two tours of duty in Afghanistan. After her time in the sandbox, she'd marked her exits and searched for anything out of the ordinary. Not that she recognized *ordinary* any-more, but she'd made it her personal goal to rediscover that quality, and she'd set herself a deadline of Christ-mas. With only three months remaining to accomplish her particular mission, scoping out potential dates—rather than potential hostiles—over bad margaritas had seemed an excellent step in the right direction. The *normal* direction.

This guy was worth a second look for many reasons, although the only threat he posed right now was to her libido. An ancient gray T-shirt stretched tightly over his shoulders as he wielded his wrench, clearly still dissat-isfied with the boat's performance despite the motor's obedient purr. He'd rolled up his faded jeans, the worn denim cupping his butt in the best possible way as he bent over, fiddling with some new mechanical bit. His dark hair was buzzed short with military precision, and his forearms were a rich, sun-browned color. When he pulled a screwdriver out of the toolbox beside him, Mia's group of gals heaved a collective sigh.

Hooyah. Definitely spectacular.

"You think he's single?" One of the bridesmaids leaned into Mia, her attention firmly fixed on the hot-tie working the engine. Laurel had assembled a bridal party from all walks of life. In addition to Mia, she'd invited two girlfriends from college, her husband-to-be's baby sister, a gal from her office and a woman she'd met on a cruise to Jamaica. Two Jenns, an Olivia, a Lily and a Chloe. Mia's *other* mission was keeping the names straight.

The guy's dating status, however, wasn't the ac-tual issue. She shifted back—she still didn't like ca-sual touching—and plucked the veil off her head. Her cousin had brought faux bridal veils for everyone, but there was only so far Mia would go for family. Being a former aviation pilot and officer in the US Army and only six months back from her final tour, pink tulle far exceeded that distance. *Far.* "That's not the right question."

The bridesmaid—Mia was *almost* certain she was one of the Jenns—absently inhaled her margarita, her gaze never wavering from the man in the boat. "No?"

A guy like him clearly didn't know the meaning of the word *no*. His T-shirt rode up as he reached over the engine block, revealing a sun-darkened expanse of golden brown skin and the navy blue edge of his boxers. The straight line of his spine just begged to be traced by her fingers. Or her mouth. Her tongue…

At ease, soldier.

She'd seen gorgeous men before. Slept with them, too. Just because sailor boy was the sexiest sight she'd laid eyes on in weeks didn't give her hormones license to rampage unchecked. Her ship sailed in hours, and she wasn't looking for quick fun. She also didn't need to leave behind yet another guy who would decide he was done waiting without telling her.

Even now, she could hear her ex's voice as he explained how her last deployment was his license to cheat on her because, honestly, did she expect him to wait forever? Eighteen months hadn't qualified as forever in Mia's book, but then honesty apparently hadn't been part of her ex's vocabulary, either. She wouldn't make that mistake again, and the sailor in the boat had *mistake* written all over his very sexy self.

Might-be-Jenn slurped, drawing Mia's attention back

to the problem at hand. "The question is—is he single right *now*?"

The man braced his legs as he twisted something on the engine block, and one of the other bridesmaids started fanning herself with a stack of bar napkins. Right on cue, a bikini-clad tourist hopped up onto the edge of the boat. The guy's fetching new visitor leaned in and said something to him.

"Scooped." Mia's neighbor polished off the remainder of her margarita. She didn't sound particularly forlorn. "I need another round."

It was hard to imagine *needing* more tequila and salt, but Mia signaled for the waiter anyhow. Her role on this cruise appeared to be that of designated party planner, probably because she wasn't any good at having fun herself, or so she suspected. Checking the waiter out visually for suspicious bulges and concealed weapons when he came over to take their order for refills was a case in point.

"Is he taken?" Bridesmaid number two—so much for keeping her vow to learn their names before the cruise ship reached international waters tomorrow—scooted closer and looked hopefully toward the water's edge.

"We could send him a drink."

"Two."

"Or bring the drinks ourselves."

"A long, slow screw against the wall." Mia zoned out during the animated discussion of drinks that followed, which was probably why she missed the right turn the conversation took somewhere between *wall* and *Mia*. Her name. Five heads swiveled her way. Hell. She must not have blacked out or had a flashback, because no one looked worried.

"What?" she asked Laurel, who was bouncing up and down in her seat. If Mia closed her eyes, she could imagine they were kids again. Laurel, who had always hated her name, had been an only child three years younger than Mia and they'd quickly become inseparable. Since her cousin lived less than a half mile away from Mia's family, there had been plenty of zipping back and forth on their bikes.

Laurel had emailed daily when Mia was deployed, sharing all the small-town news and celebrity gossip. She'd also sent care packages, which had been a mixed blessing, albeit always good for a laugh. Laurel's definition of *essentials* didn't match Mia's, but they'd agreed on chocolate and Cheetos. The random gag gifts in the box had been another matter, but explained why Mia's unit had the best supply of whoopee cushions in the sandbox…and why Mia was now sporting a hot pink bikini bottom with rhinestones. And a tiara.

Laurel had a devilish sense of humor and a contagious laugh. And since making Laurel happy made Mia happy, a little public humiliation in the wardrobe department was a small price to pay.

Laurel elbowed her. "He's wearing dog tags."

"And?"

"And so he's military, right? Maybe you know him."

Of course, because the number of soldiers serving Uncle Sam was so small that they were all on a first name basis. In the last six months she'd served in Afghanistan, she hadn't met every serviceman stationed at her base. Many of them, certainly, but not all of them. So the odds of her knowing the guy working on the boat were miniscule. Mia sighed. Sure, she could march over there and introduce herself, but she doubted he'd be interested in a glassful of vodka and gin. Sex, on the other hand, was a definite maybe if he was anything like the soldiers with whom she'd served.

Stall.

"I doubt we've crossed paths," she said, fishing an ice cube out of her glass. If she mainlined enough sweet tea, she might not fall asleep tonight, and avoiding the nightmares ranked higher on her list of things to be desired than hot men working on boats. "Afghanistan wasn't *that* small."

"Go over and ask him to join us," Laurel urged.

"Why me?"

Her cousin's impish smile reminded Mia she wasn't the only person here used to giving orders.

"I'm the bride," Laurel reminded her. As if Mia could possibly forget, given the group's collective outfits. "I'm off-limits. Taken." Another round of giggles ensued. "Someone available should go."

It was true. Mia did want to be available. It was part of her whole *act normal, feel normal* plan. Laurel, on the other hand, was unabashedly girly. She loved glitter and pink—and her husband-to-be, Jack. Laurel was the kind of happy that made others smile. She didn't forget a promise, and she'd waited almost a year for her wedding date to make sure that Mia would be home. In turn, Mia would walk through fire for her baby cousin—and up the aisle in the satin monstrosity Laurel had chosen for the bridesmaids.

All of which made walking across the beach to the hottie on the boat a no-brainer.

Since she wasn't drinking—thank you, accidentally detonated concussion grenade—she'd nominated herself to be in charge of organizing the day's festivities—kind of like a designated tour guide instead of a designated driver. They'd hit the water for some snorkeling and devoured a lunch that had somehow morphed into the current cocktails. Next up was the zip line and ATV tour, followed by a sunset beach walk. While she couldn't guarantee the bridal party's continued good behavior, she could guarantee they slept like babies tonight. Apparently, she could also add *procurer of hot men* to her mental résumé.

With that thought, she stood up and pointed herself in the direction of sailor boy. If her girls wanted his company, they'd get it. Seeing them happy was a *good* thing. This was precisely what she'd fought for in Afghanistan, this beautiful, silly happiness. Laurel glowed whenever her fiancé's name came up. They could laugh a little too loudly, drink a little too much, and have far too much fun, unlike the very few Afghani women Mia had met during her tours.

The sun beating down on the beach certainly upped the temperature to Afghanistan-like levels. Moving out without her flip-flops had been a mistake because the sand was scorching hot. As soon as Mia got close, speeding up her incoming to an undignified trot as the soles of her feet cooked, the visiting bikini babe slid off the edge of the boat, landing in the water with a little splash. Sailor boy didn't look up. Not because he didn't notice the other woman's departure—something about the way he held himself warned her he was aware of everyone and everything around him—but because polite clearly wasn't part of his daily repertoire.

Fine. She wasn't all that civilized herself.

The blonde made a face, her ponytail bobbing as she

started hoofing it along the beach. "Good luck with that one," she muttered as she passed Mia.

Oookay. Maybe this *was* mission impossible. Still, she'd never failed when she'd been out in the field, and all her gals wanted was intel. She padded into the water, grateful for the cool soaking into her burning soles. The little things mattered so much more now.

"I'm not interested." Sailor boy didn't look up from the motor when she approached, a look of fierce concentration creasing his forehead. Having worked on more than one Apache helicopter during her two tours of duty, she knew the repair work wasn't rocket science.

She also knew the mechanic and...holy hotness.

Mentally, she ran through every curse word she'd learned. Tag Johnson hadn't changed much in five years. He'd acquired a few more fine lines around the corners of his eyes, possibly from laughing. Or from squinting into the sun since rescue swimmers spent plenty of time out at sea. The white scar on his forearm was as new as the lines, but otherwise he was just as gorgeous and every bit as annoying as he'd been the night she'd picked him up at the Star Bar in San Diego. He was also still out of her league, a military bad boy who was strong, silent, deadly...and always headed out the door.

For a brief second, she considered retreating. Unfortunately, the bridal party was watching her intently, clearly hoping she was about to score on their behalf. Disappointing them would be a shame.

"Funny," she drawled. "You could have fooled me."

Tag's head turned slowly toward her. Mia had hoped for drama. Possibly even his butt planting in the ocean from the surprise of her reappearance. No such luck.

"Sergeant Dominatrix," he drawled back.

"Do you even remember my name?" Mia Brandt smiled at him, baring her teeth. If looks could kill, he'd be a dead man twice over.

Sergeant Dominatrix. Dredging up her old nickname hadn't been nice, but she'd startled him, and the words had slipped out. Okay, metaphorically speaking, she'd knocked him on his ass, because if he'd been making a list of the people he least expected to meet on Discovery Island, she would have topped said list. The last time he'd seen her had been when she'd marched out the door of his hotel room with a mouthy *At ease, soldier.* He'd been naked. She, on the other hand, had been sporting full dress uniform.

"I remember." His people-naming skills had never been good, but Mia was unforgettable.

"Prove it." She moved silently through the shallow water toward his boat. Those three feet felt like eternity.

"You don't prefer *Sergeant Dominatrix* to *Mia*?" he asked innocently.

She treated him to a repeat of the death glare, which he deserved, because it was his fault she was saddled with the nickname, even if she didn't know it. He had no intention of confessing the truth, either. He wasn't stupid.

"Would you?" she asked.

Absolutely not. He'd never been good at taking orders. Mia, on the other hand, excelled at giving them. Their relationship had been doomed from the start. Sweet Jesus, but she hadn't needed him for anything but his guy parts. At the three-drink mark of his Star Bar visit, that had been *need* enough for him.

"Touché. So…are you visiting?" See? He could be polite.

She pointed to a group of women behind her, the same group that had been mainlining cocktails and whooping it up while he worked. Funny. He wouldn't have pegged her for a drinker. Mia liked being in charge far too much to give it up.

Of course, weddings were crazy-making. He had first-hand proof of that. His business partner and best friend was tying the knot in a few months, and his fiancée had pointed out that people made allowances for weddings all the time. At the time, she'd been trying to persuade him to host some kind of stag party. This bridal party wore veils and bikinis, an unusual beach getup meriting a second glance. Or six.

Tag had never considered himself a marrying man, but multiple pink-and-white swimsuit bottoms with *bridesmaid* tattooed on the butt in rhinestones had him rethinking his position. Fast. The bride wore white, of course, and she was off-limits. The beach bar was the kind of place where the stools were chunks of wood and the glasses sported paper umbrellas and cherries. The waiters encouraged the customers to wiggle their toes in the sand and served the kind of drinks that made his stomach curdle. Mia's ladies must have come in from the cruise ship currently moored in Discovery Island's harbor, as half of them were toting *Fiesta Cruise* bags stuffed to the gills with beach towels and girly stuff.

Since the dive shop had landed a contract with the cruise ship earlier this summer, Tag knew the ship's schedule by heart. The boat would have put into port overnight, and the cruisers would have spilled down the gangway and onto the island at eight in the morning. By four o'clock, the boat would be hightailing it out of the bay, Mexico-bound. And, apparently, taking Mia along for the ride.

"Are you a matched set?" He inspected her bottom half. She'd yanked on a practical black cotton T-shirt with the US Army insignia on the upper right shoulder, but the parts of her that weren't covered up were toned and tanned. She wore her brown hair in a casual braid that fell over her shoulder as she leaned toward him. The braid was a little looser than military regulations demanded, so maybe she was taking the whole civilian thing seriously. The elegant arch of her eyebrows as she cast mental scorn in his general direction was unchanged, however, as was the alert way she balanced on the balls of her feet as if she was just waiting for a reason to kick his ass.

He had absolutely no business remembering what she looked like naked. Or just how good their one night together had been. To divert his thoughts, he peered over the side of the boat and down her body. It was his lucky day after all, because she was wearing…wait for it…a pink bikini bottom. He'd bet every dollar he had that she was bridesmaid number six.

Life was good.

"Turn around," he said, drawing the *pivot* gesture in the empty air between them with his finger. He'd never figured Mia for a rhinestone kind of woman.

Her glare promised retribution, although he found her embarrassment cute. "It's a bachelorette party. My cousin's tying the knot, and there's a dress code. Come over and have a drink with us."

And there was the Mia he remembered: all *tell* and no *ask*. A waiter delivered another round of margaritas while she waited for his response. He could practically smell the salt from the green-and-yellow slush from where he stood working on the boat's motor. The dive boat, on the other hand, smelled like sun-heated metal and motor oil, much pleasanter scents to his way of thinking. But unfortunately, the rhythmic wash of water hitting the boat's sides couldn't drown out the good-natured teasing and laughter.

"I don't believe you're active duty, Master Sergeant." He didn't know Mia's military status, but pink bikinis were no part of the military dress code he knew.

"I'm not." There was a flash of something in her eyes that he instinctively recognized. He gave her another quick once-over, this time inventorying for scars and coming up empty. Some soldiers wore their scars on the outside; others kept them on the inside. Mia was apparently an *inward* kind of person. Something he had in common with her.

"Injured?"

"I'm good. Come with me." She bit the words out impatiently, as if daring him to protest. That was fine with him. He wasn't her father, her brother or her nurse. He also wasn't a lower-ranking officer anymore due to his last promotion, which meant he absolutely didn't take orders from her. He felt the slow smile stretching his face. Oh, yeah. Master Sergeant Mia didn't get to yank his chain any longer. She was a civvie, a civilian. He, on the other hand, was still an officer and would be back with his unit in six weeks.

"Pass." He set the wrench back in the toolbox. He was about done here.

"One beer." She propped her hands on her hips and did her best to stare him down. It was a damned good effort, too, although the peekaboo bikini strap beneath her T-shirt was a first-class distraction. Her gaze never stopped moving, quartering the ocean, the boat, the beach. He'd bet she didn't miss a thing because Cal Brennan, one of the two Navy rescue swimmers he co-owned Deep Dive with, was like that, too, constantly tracking his surroundings and watching for incoming. Somehow, the switch hadn't got thrown in Tag's head. He'd left the battles on the battlefield. He was okay.

He looked over Mia's shoulder. Five pairs of eyes drilled into him from the beach bar. A lovely blonde raised her margarita to him in a silent toast, and he grinned. Pretty women on a pretty day. He should have been in heaven having things go his way like this. It was all so fun. So easy. On the other hand, there was nothing *easy* about Mia Brandt.

You had your shot and you screwed it up...

He shipped out in six weeks. She set sail in six hours. Even if he'd been a long-term kind of man, neither time line allowed for a relationship. And that assumed she even wanted him for more than a centerpiece at the bachelorette party that was in full swing up there at the beach bar.

When he didn't answer her right away, she dug in. "What's not to like about a free beer?"

He smiled. "Every drink has strings attached. I learned my lesson at the Star Bar."

She shrugged. "I didn't hear you complaining that night. In fact, you did plenty of hollering of the good kind."

Her slow smile heated his blood. He'd always loved a challenge, making him real glad he had the side of the boat between them. Otherwise, there would have been no way she missed the erection he sported. Squatting down by the side of the boat, he folded his arms on the side. The move put him on eye level with her. He'd forgotten how tiny she was.

"You made plenty of noise yourself."

"Maybe I did. A girl has to look after herself in bed." She slapped her hands on to the edge of the boat—and on top of his. She wore no rings, but there was a pale circle on her ring finger.

Ouch. He went on the offensive. "You were bossy."

She'd been bold. Confident. And more than a little take-charge in bed. So, okay, he hadn't minded at the time. He'd been completely on board with her plan of a night of hot, casual sex. And, if she'd liked to give orders, he'd also been willing to indulge her. Unfortunately, he'd been busted sneaking back into his apartment. He'd been tired. He hadn't been thinking. The litany of excuses didn't matter, however, because he'd let slip the name of the woman he'd slept with, and his night with her had solidified her reputation for being a ball-breaker.

Sergeant Dominatrix. Yeah. Not a kind name. A guy might live that down—after about four hundred tours of duty—but Mia had been a female officer working with male officers who didn't always treat women like equals, even if the field manual said they should. Good reasons, bad reasons—he figured she probably hadn't cared.

Her eyes narrowed, proving she hadn't changed since then. "You needed directions."

She was close enough to kiss. She had brown eyes, paired with the longest, most feminine eyelashes he'd ever seen. *Retreat.* His lips almost brushed hers, as his fingers automatically tightened around hers. He might be pulling her into the boat—or she might be pulling him overboard. Damned if he knew.

"Directions you were happy to issue. If you didn't like the results, you have no one to blame but yourself."

Her knowing smile pushed all his buttons. "I *was* the senior officer."

Like. Hell. "It's a good thing we were a one-night thing. Because you don't outrank me anymore, sweetheart."

2

TAG JOHNSON WAS still a pain in her ass. He was also drop-dead gorgeous. She wasn't active duty anymore. He was. The possibility he might—just possibly—outrank her galled her. She was almost certain he was teasing her.

Almost.

Big and built, he filled out a T-shirt in ways that had her libido sitting up and taking notice. Maybe it was the hint of mischief crinkling the corners of his eyes, or maybe it had something to do with his hands...yeah, his hands definitely got her going. The words tough and capable came to mind watching him work a wrench. A dive watch flashed on his wrist as he gave some unidentifiable piece of boat motor one last, hard twist and then transferred his gaze to her, thumbing his sunglasses up.

She grinned. At least she had his attention now. Taking backseat to a boat engine wasn't acceptable. She'd always had a competitive streak, and her drive to be the best had helped propel her to success in the Army. Part of it was a pilot thing—who could fly farthest, fastest, lowest. Get a bunch of aviators together, and the adjective didn't matter. She'd out-flown, out-landed, and out-shot every one of them.

Her competitive drive had been the reason why she'd met Tag in the first place. Four years ago, she'd been back stateside for a few weeks of R & R following a challenging deployment. After several weeks of parking her butt in San Diego, she'd been looking at another government-sponsored trip back to the sandbox. She'd been living dangerously for years, so sending a round of drinks over to Tag's table had seemed tame in comparison. When the waitress had brought the Mia-sponsored bonus round to his table, he'd raised his beer, laughing. See? Everyone liked a free drink. Nonetheless, she'd been completely unprepared for the bolt of pure heat shooting through her and making her think, for the first time, about indulging in the kind of one-night quickie her team boasted about. Logically, most of her guys' chatter about hookups and amazing blow-your-mind sex had to be just that. Chatter. Hot air. *Pure fiction.* Except she'd looked at Tag, and he'd stared back at her, his hazel eyes promising just one thing.

Hot.

Dirty.

Sex.

He'd made good on all those unspoken promises. They'd had just seven hours because he'd had orders to deploy in the morning. Approximately four hundred and eighteen minutes of being skin to skin with him because it had taken her two whole minutes to shuck her uniform and boots. He'd been inside her ten minutes after they'd both gotten naked, and she hadn't minded. She had, in fact, ordered him *to hurry the hell up* and *get inside me now.*

Now she stared at him as if she'd lost her ever-loving mind. Darn it. Her unfathomable attraction to him was definitely best kept on the down low.

"Earth to Mia." His husky drawl stirred more memories. He'd called her by her first name at the Star Bar, as well. She hadn't protested, despite them both knowing she outranked him. The evidence had been right there on her uniform shirt. But in her hotel room, she'd been Mia and he'd been Tag. Two people giving in to chemistry and a need for closeness before duty called and they went their separate ways.

Tag's boat rocked up and down with each small wave lapping at the beach. A familiar curl of nausea started in the pit of her stomach, so she transferred her gaze from the boat to the horizon. Throwing up on his boat would be way too humiliating.

"Are you pulling rank on me?" He was out of uniform, so she couldn't be certain he truly outranked her. Still, he'd struck her as a straight shooter, and she didn't think he'd bullshit her.

"I made Senior Petty Officer Naval Air Crewman last year."

He'd done well, but she wasn't surprised. He'd had drive. She'd certainly never had a better orgasm.

He kept on talking, or, at least, his mouth went right on moving, a small smile tugging at the corners of his lips as his eyes assessed her bikini getup, for which she definitely had to kill her cousin now. Whatever words came out, however, were lost on her as she swallowed the nausea. Her last deployment had ended with a bang, literally. While the outward damage from the concussion grenade had healed, she'd been left with an excruciating susceptibility to motion sickness. It was a good thing she'd abandoned her desire for a career as a pir-ouetting ballerina at the age of four.

He paused and looked at her. "You cashed out?"

His question, she decided, wasn't judgmental—more curious, which was a nice change. Justifying her decision to leave military service got old, as did correcting other people's misconceptions about why she'd joined in the first place. Sure the GI bill was a nice bonus, but she'd wanted to serve. Her father had. Her three brothers had. And *she* had. She got tired of people assuming she was parked in the waiting room of the VA because she was a wife or daughter.

"I'm done," she admitted.

He nodded, then turned and tossed something toward his toolbox. Instinctively, when metal hit metal with a loud bang, she dropped to a crouch. *Incoming.* Rapidly, she assessed her options for cover, mentally narrowing down the direction of the shot fired. The world telescoped to a strip of sand and the whoosh of water in her ears as she tried to pinpoint the source of the danger. The beach was still quiet and peaceful, except for her ladies sending up a rousing cheer as someone proposed a toast.

A curse floated overhead, and then Tag dropped over the side.

"Sorry." She hated the word, hated all of its implications. Her revulsion, though, didn't stop big hands from flexing, wrapping around her arm and tugging her carefully upright. She sorted through excuses halfheartedly. Maybe she'd been checking out the sand or—hey—a fish. A quick, sideways peek at Tag's face was plenty of warning. Whatever story she cooked up, he wouldn't buy it. Because he *understood*, damn him.

THE LOOK ON Mia's face was one Tag had seen on many others he'd served with. She was so busy proving she was independent and in charge that he hadn't even thought about the possibility she'd brought home some mental baggage from her tours of duty. Or that the bang of his wrench hitting the toolbox would be enough to send her back to another place and time. Another battlefield. He didn't know how to fix the situation or what she needed, but he couldn't disregard her distress, either.

"Hey." He crouched next to her, ignoring the water seeping through his jeans. He'd dry. Her eyes quartered the beach as if she fully expected a United States Marine Corps AAV to emerge from the surf and open fire. He was thankful every day Discovery Island wasn't that kind of place, but right now Mia's head didn't understand that truth.

"You're home," he murmured, not sure what words would bring her back. Carefully, he curled his fingers around her shoulder, feeling warm skin through the black cotton. It was sexy as hell. "There's no danger here."

Long lashes swept down, and she released her breath with a shudder. Had he noticed how long those lashes were when he'd had her underneath him? Or on top of him? Hell. There weren't too many positions they hadn't tried out during their one night. He'd thought she was simply a pleasant memory, but apparently he'd been wrong.

She grimaced, her eyes snapping open. She was back from whatever mental hell she'd been visiting. He dropped his hands to grip her elbows before she butt-planted in the surf. Unless she'd had a personality transplant, his Mia would want to leave with her dignity intact.

"Memories," she explained, and they both mentally added *bad* to her one-word explanation. Yeah. For one deceptive moment, she'd looked soft and vulnerable. But now, she squatted there beside his boat, ready to defend him and everyone else on the beach from invisible bad guys and…he respected the hell out of her commitment to getting the job done.

"Come on." He stood up, bringing her with him.

She'd angled herself between him and the beach like a good officer. He didn't need her to protect and defend him, but he appreciated the offer. And other things. He *definitely* appreciated Mia's body. Her butt brushed his front. Any closer and she'd be fully aware of his interest. Although she only came up to his shoulder, she looked competent and in charge, her hands on her hips as she surveyed her surroundings. Wispy strands escaped from her braid as if she'd just rolled out of bed, softening her edges. And Mia had a great many edges.

"Let me buy you a drink," she said. He didn't know whether she wanted to deflect any more questions or make sure they were even.

But did her motives matter? He could do one drink. It was hot. And he could really use a glass of water because he'd been wrestling with the damn boat motor for over an hour now. It would have been nice, though, if Mia had actually asked. Instead, like always, she was all *tell*.

And assumptions.

Not waiting for his response, she strode away from him, laying in a course for the beach bar, and the possibility of his refusing orders was clearly not an option she'd entertained. But…he'd worked around her need to be in charge four years ago. She was simply Mia and a woman he'd like to get to know just a little bit better in the very limited time he had before he shipped out again and she…got on with her own life.

So he followed her pink-and-rhinestone backside up to the beach bar. His thoughts should be illegal. Sweep his thumbs beneath the edge of her bikini. One good tug and she'd come undone.

To his chagrin, the scene at the beach bar was worse than he'd anticipated. The bride high-fived Mia as if she'd scored a hat trick and won the game for the home team, while five other women in pink rhinestone bikinis eyed him assessingly. Hell. This was not a drink with an old Army buddy. This was an interrogation. Or the dating version of musical chairs.

"Sit there." Mia pointed at the single empty seat beside a blond bridesmaid who looked as though she'd just won the lottery. At least they were color-coded. Pink for available and white for completely off-limits. He sat down in what he was fairly certain was Mia's seat, but he wasn't completely sure how he'd ended up here.

Mia made the introductions, then waved down a waiter and placed an order for another round of drinks. The two of them were the only ones going with iced tea today. He watched her effortlessly organize her bridesmaid troop. In some ways, she was just the same as before, giving orders, arranging things. With the best of intentions—he'd give her that. She wasn't bossy just to be take-charge. It was simply that she was a planner and not afraid to assume command. Ever. In under five minutes, she had the drink orders marshaled, seats rearranged, and the conversational train headed in a pleasant direction.

"You're active duty?" The bridesmaid next to him toyed with the dog tags around his neck. He put a few more inches of space between them, although there wasn't much room to retreat. His leg bumped the bare thigh of the bride on the other side. *Coward* he mouthed at Mia. She'd stuck to her post on the far side of the group.

She grinned, a gleeful smile illuminating her face at his discomfort. Whoa. Her happiness was a one-two punch to his gut. *Don't think about what it felt like to be deep inside her.* Good luck with that. Maybe she'd acquired mind-reading skills in her last deployment, because her smile widened. Instead of being all serious and take-charge, Sergeant Dominatrix had a fun side. Who knew?

"I'm helping out a buddy on the island. He's launching a dive business and needed a few extra hands on deck. I'm active duty in six weeks."

Which he hadn't planned on doing when he'd first come out to Discovery Island. Not re-upping had been a done deal. And then he'd gotten a call from his team leader, asking for one more mission, one more deployment. He'd thought he'd picked a spot, decided to settle down. But he was…bored. His feet itched to go somewhere, anywhere. Air Rescue Swimmers didn't just rescue the drowning. They also conducted surveillance in drug ops and ran recovery missions. Their CO needed someone with his skills—and Discovery Island *didn't* need him. Daeg Ross could hire any other vet and that was the truth. He'd stick it out until the replacement guy showed up, and then he'd haul ass back to San Diego and his real job.

"Doing what?" His pink-and-rhinestone inquisitor scooted closer.

Keep it simple. "I'm a Navy rescue swimmer."

Mia leaned across the table. "He picked up our pieces. If a pilot went down, Tag and his unit went in. They fished us out of the water. Bad storm, tsunami, sinking boat—they were our go-to guys."

College had been as far out of reach for his eighteen-year-old self as a trip to the moon or Outer Mongolia. A week after his high school graduation, he'd enlisted. He'd completed two years of training in advanced swimming and lifesaving techniques, then deployed to his first squadron. He knew his weapons and tacticals, but his job had been rescuing people. He'd never been a combatant.

Unlike Mia.

She'd been fierce, a fighter in bed and out. The night they'd met, she'd been a fish out of water, sending him drinks at the bar and then looking insulted when he returned the gesture. Normally, he would have avoided a woman like her. After training hard, fighting tooth and nail for each rescue, he wanted a simple, uncomplicated hookup. But he hadn't been able to keep away from Mia. Had instead followed her home when she'd looked over her shoulder at him and said *come*. Nothing about her had been relaxing or fun, but he hadn't minded. Had, in fact, been hooked.

The bride looked at the two of them, her head snapping left, then right, as if she was watching a tennis match at Wimbledon. "You two know each other?"

Biblically.

"Mia bought me a drink once." He tipped his head toward the former sergeant.

Who grinned right back at him. "And he was worth it. Best seven dollars I ever dropped in a bar."

The bride shook her head. "Who knew you'd meet up again on Discovery Island?"

Who knew indeed? The iced tea level in his glass sank to the halfway point. The overabundance of sugar had his teeth curdling. "How long are you ladies in town for?"

The bride checked her phone. "Five more hours."

Her face glowed as she inundated him with endless, incomprehensible details about her wedding in two months, and which families were flying from where. In his line of work, Tag had saved other people's families. His first rescue had sent him a picture a couple of weeks after Tag had fished the guy out of the Pacific Ocean: the man had gone home, and his daughter had sent a photo of the two of them dancing at her wedding. That was a good picture, a good day.

While he made polite chitchat, he was aware of Mia getting up. She moved around the group, identifying drink recipients for the waiter with smooth efficiency. Alcoholic beverages sorted, she returned to the bride and produced a tube of sunscreen with an SPF of about a million and one.

"Strapless dress. Time to lather up."

The bride obediently presented her back, and Mia got to work spreading the sunscreen over her bare shoulders. Slick with lotion, her hands slid up the tanned expanse of the bride's back, then back down again... and, hello, hard-on.

Perfect. That was his cue. He stood up to leave and did his best to pretend bridesmaid number four hadn't just patted his butt. Plausible deniability. Mia apparently had plenty of imagination herself, because she kept sliding him covert glances. She was good. He doubted any of her friends had noticed her interest.

He had.

He brushed past her, paused. "You need to stop staring."

Chairs crowded their table at the beach bar, leaving limited room to maneuver. Instead of easing away from him, she lost her balance in the sand and made full body contact, her breasts pressed against his bare arm. One cotton T-shirt. One pink bikini top. There was nowhere near enough fabric between them.

She leaned back and folded her arms over her chest. Too bad. He'd been enjoying the contact. "I'm not. Staring. At you."

"Uh-huh." *Rattled* was also a new condition for Mia. He'd seen her aroused and take-charge. *Coming.* Which was his personal favorite, because that was the closest she came to really letting go and…he needed to stop remembering. Right now. He nodded his head in the general direction of the bridal party. "Ladies. Thank you."

Mia followed him of course, her flip-flops snapping loudly against the sand.

"Explain," she demanded.

He flashed a smile at her, loving the way her fingers curled into her bare arms. He got to her. No matter what words came out of her prickly, sassy mouth, she wasn't indifferent to him. At all.

"Remember—you don't outrank me." The unspoken *anymore* hung in the air between them. Yeah, spending time with Mia would be dangerous. He couldn't afford a two-night stand with her, and she didn't have room in her life for a man like him.

As soon as Tag retreated, Mia's ladies declared themselves ready to move on. Go figure. They'd been holding out for man candy, and, now that they'd had their taste, they were good. She stared after Tag's mighty fine backside disappearing down the boardwalk. Worn denim cupped tight buns, hugging him in all the right places. She'd hung on to his butt, digging her fingers into the hard muscles as he worked himself... Shoot. He was right. She *was* staring.

"What's next? Or should I ask—who?" Her cousin grinned happily at her.

Yeah. She had the same question. With five bridesmaids and one bride staring at her, however, she needed to pull it together. Her brief past with Tag Johnson was her own business, and discovering he'd somehow ended up on the same island as her—however briefly—was not something she *needed* to share. In fact, forgetting all about his sexy butt topped her current to-do list. She'd get right on it.

When her cousin stood up, the other women fell in behind her like baby ducks. Then they all turned and stared expectantly at Mia. Right. Because somehow she'd ended up in charge of this zoo. She consulted her iPad where she had their action plan for the day. Beach bar? Check. Next up was zip-lining.

Oh, joy.

Mia snuck one last look down the boardwalk, but Tag had disappeared. The boardwalk teemed with activity in the late afternoon sunshine with tourists strolling up and down in the palm tree–studded shade. Discovery Island appealed to her on a fundamental level. The place was pretty. It had palm trees. But, more importantly, the locals seemed friendly, and she'd bet there was just about zero crime. Whatever. Their cruise ship floating on the horizon was plenty of reminder. Five hours until departure.

Her own wistful sigh was irritating as heck.

Snap out of it. It wasn't as if anything could have come of her chance encounter with Tag. A hot one-night fling didn't mean he was up for a repeat performance. Or that she wanted one herself. Nope. She'd had her fun, and now she had a bachelorette party to lead. She motioned for the group to move out.

"Who's ready for some zip-lining?"

3

Throwing up on a public beach was rude. But Mia's stomach wasn't on board with being polite, the pounding headache building between her eyes demanded relief of one kind or another. She'd captured some great pictures of her cousin with the mock veil. The ATV ride had gone well. But the zip line...big mistake.

One of their guides had thought it would be fun to encourage them to spin upside down, and his impulsive gesture had triggered an episode of motion sickness she'd really rather forget. If she'd only stayed upright, her prescription would have continued to do its job. Instead, the overzealous guide had given her meds a workout her head couldn't handle.

Not ready to confront a world that rocked violently up and down, she kept her eyes screwed shut. The rustle of palm fronds overhead was actually somewhat soothing. If she was lucky—and, given the way her day had gone so far, she probably shouldn't be investing in lottery tickets—the darned tree wasn't sporting any coconuts. Her head simply couldn't take any more knocks.

She waited for a moment for the universe to weigh in, but her life remained coconut-free. Good times.

"Mia?" Her cousin's voice floated through the darkness, demanding attention. A hand squeezed her shoulder.

"That's me," she muttered.

"Are you okay?"

No. She absolutely, positively wasn't.

"I'm going to head back to the boat and sleep off this headache," she said instead. No way was she ruining her cousin's day. "You guys finish up your shopping and I'll meet you on the main deck for dinner."

Tomorrow.

But there was no way she'd make it back on board without an assist right now. She could lie here. Work on her siesta skills. Maybe, if she closed her eyes for a few minutes, she wouldn't need a helping hand from the boat's crew. And there were worse things than taking a short nap beneath a palm tree, right?

"Are you sure?"

"You bet."

"You want me to take your things for you?" Bags rustled.

"That would be great," she groaned. *Anything you want. Just go.*

Ten minutes and a quick siesta.

All she needed was time to settle her stomach, and then she'd be good as new.

THE THUNDERSTORM MOVING toward Discovery Island had painted the last visible portions of the sky an ominous purple. The Fiesta cruise ship was a tiny white blob on the horizon…taking Mia and any chance of a reunion hookup with it. Temptation removed.

Even though Discovery Island wasn't really his kind of place, Tag had to admit the evening scene was a fun one. Tourists strolled down the boardwalk, debating dinner options and enjoying the sea breeze. None of them looked at the horizon and weighed the possibility of a rescue call against the height of the waves and the distance to the ocean's surface. He loved his job, and the siren call of the storm building on the horizon promised action and a good fight. When the rain and the waves hit, wreaking their usual havoc, the island would need him. He'd have things to do.

Sitting still and watching wasn't his thing, because he didn't run with the vacation crowd anymore than he did with the casserole crowd. The avid interest of Discovery Island's long-term residents in his dating life was off-putting. To say the least. The attention shouldn't have bothered him since he was used to living life in a fishbowl. But Discovery Island was a small place, and some days it felt more like he was a tasty squid swimming in a shark tank at a very public aquarium. Even the rescue-ops part of the job had dating perils—his last rescue, the eighty-one year-old Ellie Damiano, was *still* trying to set him up with her granddaughter.

Somehow, the things he rescued always stuck to him. Sure, he might have wrapped an arm around Mrs. Damiano and talked with her. But what other choice did he have? She'd just driven her car off the road and into two feet of water. She'd needed an ear to bend, and he had two perfectly good ones. He'd listened. And listened. And then listened some more. He swore, Mrs. Damiano had more to say than anyone he'd ever met before.

Now she was grateful, wanting to do something nice for him, and he didn't have the heart to turn that down.

He just didn't want to go out with her granddaughter.

As the last few sunbathers packed it in, vacating the creamy strip of sand between the boardwalk and the surf, he turned away from the radar showing only empty waters around Discovery Island—no enemy hostiles or floundering commercial liners or even a capsized fishing boat—and got down to business. The sooner he said the words, the sooner he could get on with what needed doing, so he turned back to face the two men in Deep Dive's command center. He'd served with both Daeg and Cal for multiple tours of duty, but the bond between them was more than a shared set of missions. There was no one he'd trust more with his back, and each of them had stood by the others on rescues.

"I re-upped." Short and sweet. A declarative sentence rather than a question, because his going back to San Diego wasn't open for negotiation.

Cal looked up from the mountain of paper on his desk and cursed. "Don't tell me. This is Mrs. Damiano's fault. You could try going out with her granddaughter and see if a date stops her."

The man had five-o'clock shadow at midafternoon and a pyramid of Red Bull cans teetering in front of him. He'd been the one to conceive of the dive business in the first place, convinced the small California island where he'd grown up was in desperate need of an adventure diving outfit. Plus, he'd taken on the task of setting up a search-and-rescue program for the area. The local Coast Guard was overwhelmed and focused more on running down drug traffickers than fishing distressed pleasure boaters out of the water. Cal, of course, was committed to keeping everyone safe. Juggling both meant less sleep for everyone, although his buddy had never complained.

Reaching over, Tag swiped a stack of papers from Mount Paperwork. Cal didn't protest. The first one was an invoice for emergency supplies, but the second was for parts for the chopper. Lots and lots of parts. Lovely. They needed a mechanic. Or stock in an aviation company. Their used bird was a work in progress with more face-lifts than an aging beauty queen. The chopper was also an *expensive* work in progress, as Cal liked to point out with annoying frequency. Restoration had been Tag's responsibility, in between running dives and setting up training exercises. Apparently, he should have made time for bookkeeping. Or kidnapping an accountant.

"I can handle Mrs. Damiano." *Not.* The old woman redefined *determined.* "Our CO needs a pilot," he said, when the silence stretched on too long.

Daeg signed a check and shoveled papers into an envelope. "You're not the only sailor who knows how to fly a bird or run a rescue op," he pointed out.

True enough. The Spec Ops boys were planning on taking out a drug op in South America, however, and their CO knew the mission would hit a personal hot spot with Tag. Passion counted, because a soldier who took the mission personally would go the extra mile every time.

Passion aside, he was also pretty much the only man available at the moment. "He asked. Most of the other guys are already assigned. I'm not."

Cal cracked a new can of Red Bull, tipping it in Tag's direction. "Cheers, then."

Mission accomplished, Tag kept right on sorting, circling and adding invoices. Maybe before he went away, he'd post on craigslist for an office manager. The silence built up until Tag was itching to move. But he had more numbers to add, and shoving the pile back on to Cal's desk wasn't happening. The guy was exhausted.

He grabbed a stamp, peeled and stuck. "We need help. Office help."

"Speak for yourself." Cal flipped Tag the bird. "Because I'm doing just fine here, and Dani's going to be helping us out in a month or two."

Daeg grinned. "She estimates another two to three weeks. Just long enough for us to get really desperate."

Dani Andrews, Daeg's fiancée, was an actuary and damned good with numbers. She was in the process of setting up a freelance business on the island, but she was currently snowed under with clients. She'd promised to help out just as soon as she could clear the decks, and bringing her on board would be great. The heap of papers on Cal's desk listed sideways, and Cal cursed, making a grab for the topmost invoices as Mount Paperwork toppled over and hit the floor.

"Right. Or maybe we can't wait."

Cal scooped up the papers and deposited them back on the desk. Shoving to his feet, he prowled toward the front of the dive center. The air was thick outside, vibrating with tension as the purple clouds swept closer and closer toward the island.

Cal stared outside with the same kind of longing Tag felt. "Storm's moving in."

"Not a bad one." The thunderstorm headed their way was the usual summer fare. It would bring plenty of heat and some flash-bang. It wasn't the kind, however, that led to flooding and rescue calls. He could go home and crash. This would be a quick, wet, *loud* summer storm, but the property damage would be minimal, and no one would be getting hurt. No one would need him tonight.

A good night.

The wind was picking up, whipping the tops of the palms back and forth. The beach was all but deserted now, except for a single woman leaning against a palm, seemingly asleep. She wore a navy blue sweatshirt, the hood pulled up over her head, and a pair of cotton shorts that hugged her butt and left her long, tanned legs on display. Maybe she was grabbing a last moment of toes-in-the-sand fun or maybe she was waiting for someone. "You're staring." Cal punched him in the shoulder.

Maybe. But he wasn't responsible for where his eyes went when he was thinking. Some things actually were beyond his control. Kind of like his one night with Mia, his head—and another body part—reminded him. His lack of control should have embarrassed him, but she'd been right there with him. He'd never been one for picking women up at a bar, but for Mia he'd made an exception, and he still wasn't sure why. Not because she was gorgeous—although she was and that had certainly helped persuade him—but for some other reason he couldn't put into words.

"I'm staring at the beach," he countered. *Liar.*

"A beach with women on it." Daeg said, coming up behind them. He'd met his fiancée on Discovery Island when a bad tropical storm had sent him out to rescue her from a flooding Jeep. Tag didn't need or want to know what had happened when the pair had holed up to wait out the storm, but he'd seen the ring—and he'd seen the look on Daeg's face. The man had fallen, and fallen hard.

Tag raised a brow, because no way he was letting Daeg off easily. "Now you're looking, too."

A small smile tugged at his friend's lips. Yeah…they were both busted. "I'm not dead."

No, but Daeg was disgustingly happy with the soon-to-be Mrs. Ross. Although Tag strongly suspected the bride would keep her own name. Independent, strong-minded and fun, Dani was the perfect woman for Daeg, and Tag was happy for them. He really was. He knew he sported a big-ass grin whenever he thought about the two of them and this place. Discovery Island had the heart of a small town, a heart he recognized. He'd been born and raised in Rutland, Vermont. In his small New England town, plenty of people knew his name and his business. You kissed a girl, and every relative, every member of her church, started looking for commitment and a ring. So far, Discovery Island had been a good station. It certainly wasn't fighting a losing battle against street drugs.

Not that Rutland was any kind of inner city ghetto with urban blight on display on every corner. Nope. The clapboard houses in his hometown were run-down some, but when the snow fell or the leaves changed, pretty enough. The problem had been the baggies of drugs flowing in from urban centers, marked up and selling fast. He'd had friends boast about fortunes made selling heroin they'd bought off the runners who made daily trips from New York City to Vermont.

More than one of his high school friends had kept hidden stashes of cash, guns and drugs, tooling around in an SUV and making deals. Just blue-collar folks sucked into a morass of drugs and all the accompanying bad shit. It was your neighbor breaking into your house and boosting your electronics because he was jonesing for a fix and flat broke. Tag had lost a girlfriend to drug addiction. He'd stuck it out for as long as possible, but then he'd finally had to let go. He had a feeling, though, Daeg was going to have the happy ending.

"You'll be a dead man if Dani catches you eyeing the scenery." A grin split Cal's face.

"Right." Daeg rocked back on his heels. "And Piper won't mind at all if you're looking at other women."

Cal held up a hand. "Hey, you started it. I'm just finishing things here. Closing the loop. Making sure you all behave."

Right. While Cal and Daeg bickered amicably, Sleeping Beauty woke up. Levering herself away from the tree and grabbing her towel, she wrapped the blue-and-white stripes around her like a cloak, bent over and threw up. Then she curled into a small ball, as if even the thought of moving was too much. He knew the feeling, but he also knew the skies were close to opening up and drenching the beach. She couldn't stay where she was. She'd either be brained by errant coconuts or drowned.

Maybe she was drunk.

Or had some kind of virulent bird flu.

Whatever her issue, it wasn't his problem. Still, when she heaved again, his own gut twinged in sympathy. Daeg frowned, and Tag didn't have to look over at Cal to know the other man's face reflected a similar concern. None of them could walk past a civilian in need of a rescue.

"She need an assist?" Cal fished his cell phone out of his pocket, clearly running possible rescue missions through his head.

"Ouch." Daeg winced sympathetically as the subject of their attention hunched over, looking more miserable by the second.

Surely someone would show up and lead her off. She couldn't be here by herself. One set of dry heaves later, however, and she was still alone. Damn it.

Daeg hummed a few bars of the *Lone Ranger* theme music. "He's going to do it."

Cal looked at him. "Yep."

Tag didn't even have to ask. "Someone has to rescue her. You two could volunteer."

"Sure, but we don't have to," Cal admitted cheerfully. "We've got you to go in for us. Plus, you're the only one who's still single, just in case she's like Mrs. Damiano and decides *rescue service* is a synonym for *dating service*."

Daeg hesitated. The guy's white-knight complex would get him into serious trouble someday. *Pot meet kettle.* "You'll take care of her?"

"Yeah." Joking aside, it went without saying none of them would leave a woman alone on a beach in distress. Since he was the only one who didn't have someone waiting at home for him, he figured that made him tonight's rescuer elect. "I've got her."

"If you need help—" Again, some things didn't have to be said.

He flipped Cal the bird. "I'm good. Go get on with your life. Kiss Piper for me. Have some fun."

He strode down the boardwalk, hung a left and crunched his way out onto the sand. Yeah, he liked his combat boots because, sue him, the military gave good boot. Part of him thought rushing to the lady's rescue was a stupid idea, but then she made a small sound of distress and finished unloading the contents of her stomach on the palm tree next to his bike. Okay, scratch that.

She needed help.

Five feet away and closing fast, he spotted a flash of pink. Which could have been a coincidence. Plenty of women had pink swimsuits, and the last female he'd seen in a pink swimsuit was supposed to be on a cruise ship at sea. Not here.

Two feet out, he scuffed the sand because he didn't want to add a heart attack to the woman's woes. She had the towel pulled up over her head like a cloak, one sun-tanned arm braced against the sand. This close, he could read the word *bridesmaid* on her arm where someone had written it in sunscreen. It was the kind of practical joke he'd play on Daeg—or that Mia's bridesmaids might have thought up. *Damn it.*

Please, please, don't let her be here.

SOMEONE LARGE AND MALE crouched down beside her. Usually, Mia would have taken defensive measures, but right now she was too miserable to care. The world swung in dizzying circles, making her stomach lurch up and down.

"Mia?" Okay. She cared. She recognized that deep growly voice. Tag was back.

Don't groan because you might puke on his feet. "I already bought you a thank-you drink. Don't you ever go away?"

He pressed a bottle of cold water into her hand, and,

okay, she might have moaned. Even if he couldn't be bought off with beverages, apparently she could.

"All the time. In fact, I have a date with Uncle Sam in six weeks. Rinse and spit."

To her eternal shame, she did as he ordered. He measured her pulse, then tilted her head back to check her pupils. She let him because, right now, she was too wiped out to fight. If Tag had apparently decided to become her very own EMT tonight, she'd work with him. Tomorrow was plenty of time to take issue with his high-handed behavior.

"Follow my finger," he said gruffly, moving his finger first left, then right. "Alcohol? Bird flu? Bad run-in with a zip line?"

His face was close to hers. Kissing distance, in fact, although she bet kissing was the last thing on his mind right now. His eyes were hazel with gold flecks, something she either hadn't noticed or had forgotten. Huh. Her Senior Chief had pretty eyes.

"Zip line," she muttered, when he let the silence stretch on.

"How?" Brow furrowing with concern, he immediately started palpating her arms as if he feared she'd somehow fallen off the zip line and then crawled to the beach to lick her wounds.

"Geez." She knocked his hands away. "I didn't fall off the thing. I just got dizzy."

He rocked back on his heels. "You're motion sick?"

"Got it in one."

He eased her upright. "Okay. Deep breath."

"I know what to do."

"Uh-huh. This happens often?"

When he turned her forearm over, she spotted the *bridesmaid* temporarily tattooed on her skin.

"I owe someone for that." Probably her cousin. It was exactly the kind of thing Laurel would do.

"Let's focus on you right now." Tag slid his thumbs down her wrist and pushed on a spot. "Give me ten," he said, when she tried to yank her arm away.

Leaning backward against him, supported by the strong column of his thighs, was no hardship. Her fingers flexed, finding denim. Shoot. There was nothing professional about this, although he didn't seem to mind.

"How were you injured?" He sounded matter-of-fact, but she'd bet he wouldn't be happy if she trotted out all of *his* vulnerabilities with a cheery *let's discuss*.

"Uncle Sam and the call of duty. Now, go away." The words sounded childish, but she didn't care. The world wasn't swinging quite so badly anymore, the nausea dissipating now that her stomach had emptied itself. Yeah, the worst was over, but she was so not winning any prizes for elegance. Good thing she wasn't still attracted to Tag.

"You don't really want me to leave." Amusement colored his deep voice.

"And you'd be wrong. Ask me why."

His hand rubbed a small, lazy circle against the back of her neck, and the water bottle returned to her mouth. "Small sip."

"Why are you here?"

"Because you threw up on my motorcycle." She followed his pointing finger, and, sure enough, there was a big black Harley parked beside her palm tree haven. She'd missed his tires. Score one for her. "And because you need help."

"You make a career out of rescuing damsels in distress? And, for the record, I didn't hit your bike." She sounded bitchy. She knew that. Accepting help, however, was out of the question. She stood on her own two feet. Or, she admitted wryly, lay on her own butt. Whatever it took. With her brothers and her father all being active duty, bitchy had been the only way to hold her own. Give them an inch and they'd smother her with love and concern. Of course, Tag wasn't offering love, but, still…she had this. She'd led a team in Afghanistan until she'd retired, so handling a bout of motion sickness was child's play.

"You want to ask me why I'm so certain you need help?" His calm voice annoyed her, she decided. As did the supreme confidence with which he moved his hands over her body. She just might live, however, thanks to his nifty acupressure trick. Two inches down her wrist and press hard. She could do that.

She took a good look around her, expanding her world beyond the sand, the man and the Harley. Post-sunset shadows painted the sand with stripes of dark. The cruise ship sailed at five o'clock. The beach around her had emptied out, and the sun was no more than a red-orange sliver above the horizon. And…no ocean liner bobbing away on the water or even anywhere to be seen. She asked the obvious question, even though she knew what the answer was going to be. *Too late. You snooze, you lose.*

"What time is it?"

"Seven." He extended the wrist with the dive watch so she could see for herself.

"They sailed without me." Her brain tried to kick into planning mode, but a bout of motion sickness always wiped her out, leaving her fuzzy-headed. Finishing her siesta here on the beach had sounded like a decent enough plan—she could figure things out in the morning.

"No public camping on the beach," he said pleasantly, as if he'd read her mind. "Go ahead and say it. It won't kill you."

"Fine. Can you recommend a hotel for the night?" The emergency twenty bucks and the cell phone she'd shoved in her shorts pocket wouldn't take her far. She'd have to call for cash and new cards. Rejoining the cruise was probably not feasible—the ship was headed down the California coast for a quick pit stop in Ensenada, Mexico, and then to Cabo, where everyone would get off and fly home. By the time she made it to an airport, her cousin would already be airborne.

"Mia." She felt rather than saw him shake his head. "That's not happening. You can spend the night with me."

"I'm fine."

Liar.

Her gaze dropped to his hands. His strong, capable hands that were holding her up because otherwise she was likely to butt-plant on the sand. She hated feeling weak. Hated *being* weak.

"You can't stay here," he said, using his calm, logical voice again. She wondered what it would take to get him angry and loud. "You're sick. You're homeless. And, since I don't see a purse, I suspect you're broke, as well."

"You certainly know how to lift a girl's spirits."

He kept right on talking. "So, the way I see it, you need a place to fall back to for the night."

He was right, damn him. She chewed on her lower

lip as she thought her situation through. Twenty bucks simply didn't go far, and she didn't have so much as an ID with her because her cousin had taken Mia's purse back to the ship. Tag didn't say anything as he waited for her to come to the obvious conclusion.

"Are you going to make me say it?"

His sigh ruffled her hair. "Yes, Mia, I am."

Problem was, she was best at *giving* orders. Not taking them. He didn't say anything else, though, and he was right, damn it. She needed somewhere to spend the night, she was temporarily broke and she knew him.

"Take me home with you." She wouldn't, couldn't say *please*.

"You got it." He rose smoothly, setting her back on her own two feet. So why, if he'd given her exactly what she'd wanted, did she feel disappointed?

4

Tag's place was a short walk from the beach. It figured a Navy man would want to be near the water. What she hadn't expected was the picture-pretty complex of little apartments built for one. The place screamed cute, starting with the courtyard filled with tropical plants and a hot-pink fuchsia shrub going crazy. Tag headed straight for the first place on the left, unlocked a set of glass French doors and then hesitated. She really hoped he wasn't about to rescind his invitation, because she was tired enough now to beg. Tomorrow was soon enough to sort out the crazy mess her life had become.

He looked down at her, where she was plastered up against his side pretending this was a voluntary closeness rather than him holding her up. "You don't mind animals, do you?"

Right now, she'd kill for a pillow and a bed. "Is that a euphemism?"

She was only willing to take this white knight thing so far, although she'd even consider trading sexual favors for a toothbrush right now. Whatever he was asking, though, was lost when one of his neighbors—an

elderly one from the quavering sound of the voice—
bellowed out his window at them in a voice that was
probably audible back on the beach.

"Is she your girlfriend? Hot damn!"

Wow. Tag got around. She leaned against him harder.
"Girlfriend?"

Tag blushed, dark color staining his cheeks. Holy
moly. She didn't know the man had it in him. "Mr. Brad-
ley may be under a mistaken impression."

Uh-huh. She'd just bet.

"That's Mr. *Bentley* to you. Check my mailbox next
time you forget my name."

"Either you have a girlfriend or you don't." She might
have been out of the dating pool for a few years, but
even she knew that much. Tag muttered something, taking the high road, and shoved the doors open. Whatever. She'd be the first to admit her social skills were
rusty. She waved in Mr. Bentley's general direction and
followed Tag inside. He wasn't much on furniture—he
had a couch and a coffee table and nothing else—but a
fifty-pound bag of dog food dwarfed the kitchen counter. The bag of cat food next to it wasn't much smaller,
completely overshadowing a couple of browning ba-
nanas. Maybe he had monkeys, too, because the man
clearly had hidden depths.

"You have pets," she said, stating the obvious as a
white boxer wearing a happy grin loped toward them,
followed by a Chihuahua suffering from some kind of
eye infection. A geriatric cat and a rabbit brought up
the rear of the parade. Honest to God, the man had his
own Easter bunny, even if he'd apparently passed on
the monkeys.

She hazarded a random guess because it had been

a day full of surprises. "You've become a vet because rescue swimming is so boring."

"No." He greeted the dogs and the cat, picking up the rabbit and tucking it beneath his arm. Tag's place was definitely small. He had a teeny living room and a galley kitchen too miniscule to hold the two of them. "Meet Ben Franklin, Buckeye, Beauregard, and Cadbury. Cadbury's the one with the floppy ears, in case you're wondering, but they're all boys, and no one comes when called. The bathroom's through there," he said, waving a hand toward the hall.

"Are you moonlighting as Doctor Doolittle?" Snarking distracted her from the residual queasiness in her stomach—and the awkwardness of being here, alone with him, when she had memories of him naked. "Why all the animals?"

He shrugged, a powerful roll of his shoulders. "They needed a place."

She settled for escaping into the bathroom while he fed his menagerie. The man even had a bonus toothbrush, which after her palm-tree encounter, she was pathetically grateful for. Mint had never tasted so good—and was all she wanted to taste right now. Not a big, too-charming, badass Navy man who thought she needed rescuing. No way, no how.

TAG HAD RENTED the apartment furnished from Mr. Bentley, and taking things month-to-month had seemed wise. Now with his plans to leave Discovery Island firmed up, the decision was even more fortunate. It wasn't like he owned any furniture anyhow. He'd always traveled light, and his non-ops stuff fit in a pair of duffel bags. So he shouldn't have this strange, warm *feeling* of satisfaction, getting Mia on his turf. The first time—the *last* time, he reminded himself—they'd gone at it in her hotel room. The place had been perfectly comfortable, and they'd really only been interested in the bed. The wall. He grinned slyly. And the floor...

The boxer bumped his leg, making himself known. "Lucky dog."

Ben Franklin panted happily up at him, everything right in his doggie world.

Tag's own life wasn't quite as simple, and Mia was just the latest symptom. He was a sucker for four-legged and lonely. He'd have to figure something out, though, before he headed back to San Diego in six weeks. Base housing wouldn't allow animals, and, although he could rent a place off base, finding a pet-friendly landlord would be a challenge. And, besides, animals couldn't be left alone for months on end. Somehow, he needed to re-home the menagerie in the next six weeks. He definitely shouldn't have named them.

Buckeye gave him a reproachful glare, as if he'd read Tag's mind and knew the guy who provided the dog chow was having second thoughts. Or getting attached. Yeah. It was the *attached* part that posed a problem.

"We should get her a shirt, yeah?" One way or another, he'd figure out a solution to his animal woes. Maybe Dani need a dog. Or two. And Piper was definitely a cat person.

Beauregard rubbed against his ankles, decorating his jeans with cat hair, and then pranced down the hallway, tail swishing. The haughty gesture looked enough like a *yes* to him, so he took his cue and followed the tail. Thank God he'd done laundry this week. Mia had served overseas, and she'd have roughed it more than once, but even he drew the line at offering her a used T-shirt.

After grabbing a clean shirt, he fell back down the hallway and rapped on the bathroom door. The sound of water running got his imagination going. She could be naked in there. Naked and wet. She had a gorgeous body, all toned, tanned lines and feminine strength. He could… He didn't know what he could do. *Hell.*

The water stopped, followed by the sounds of movement inside. Had he left a towel in there? Damn. He had no idea, but he was no Martha Stewart. If he was lucky, he had toilet paper and a toothbrush. The door cracked, and Mia stared through the small space. She still sported the purple shadows underneath her eyes, but her color was better. Maybe her stomach was finally settling down.

"What?"

Yeah. What? He was standing and staring. He yanked his attention back to the job at hand and waved the shirt at her. "Wardrobe change."

She grabbed his peace offering, which meant she had to open the door farther. Bingo. He had his opening. He should move back. Give her space. Instead, he curled a hand around the frame and inserted a foot into the crack she'd created. She was fully dressed, although she smelled like mint and hand soap. He stared at her while she turned his offering over in her hands and examined it.

"You're giving me a Navy T-shirt?" She looked up at him, her eyes laughing. How had he missed her sense of humor? She'd also unbraided her hair, and the loose waves made her look softer. Younger. Okay…it also made her look tousled and fresh out of bed, so the new hairstyle wasn't a good thing because it gave him too many ideas.

He'd grabbed the first clean T-shirt he'd found and, yeah, it might also have been the *only* clean shirt in his possession at the moment. Beggars, choosers and all that. If she didn't like her choice, she could wear her own things or go naked. Naked definitely worked for him.

He shrugged, as if some small part of him didn't like the thought of her wearing his shirt. "The shirt's optional."

She wasn't looking at the clothing, though—instead, she was staring at him and, more specifically, at his *mouth*. How was he supposed to be a gentleman? She was a *veteran*. Injured. And breathtaking. He was going to hell, but he wanted his own brand of sensual revenge. She'd pulled rank on him during their one night in San Diego, and he...well, he'd been willing to let her. Not this time. This time he had plans—if he was being honest with himself—for erotic payback.

"Open the door or close it." He growled the words, no longer interested in playing nice. His voice sounded rough and harsh to his own ears and, oh yeah, *needy*. While she, on the other hand, had made it perfectly clear she didn't need him so much. He was a place to stay and a toothbrush, although she could have taken care of the problem on her own. Even puking on the beach, Mia was frighteningly competent.

He moved a step nearer, his fingers digging into the door frame. He was close enough to feel the heat coming off her body, to smell his soap on her skin. She was sexy as hell, but this night wasn't supposed to be about sex. He let go of the door, but he didn't back up, didn't fall back down the hallway and put some space between them. Instead he got closer—and damned if she didn't help him. She moved toward him in a sweet collision. Her breasts crushed against his chest, her thighs pressed against his. All those layers of clothes couldn't keep him from remembering what she'd felt like naked in his arms.

And wanting a repeat.

Keeping his hands off her was impossible. So he clasped a hand around the back of her neck, tracing the soft skin, loving how the small tendrils of hair clung to his fingers as he drew her closer. She made a small, throaty sound, tipping her head back against the door, and he was lost.

He covered her mouth with his and kissed her. She was warm and soft and, as his tongue tangled with hers because she kissed with as much certainty as she did everything else, he felt the strangest sense of coming home. They'd kissed before, dozens of times, during their one post–Star Bar night, but the reality was even better than his memories. She slid her hands up his arms and over his shoulders, grabbing his shirt and palming the back of his head.

He wanted her, every stubborn, prickly and sensuous inch of her.

Never mind they were both leaving and he probably had no business touching her without admitting to his part in her unwelcome nickname. Or that he'd brought her here because she was sick and alone, which made kissing her a bastard move. Instead of stopping, though, he deepened their kiss, tasting mint and Mia. Damn it. Toothpaste shouldn't be such a turn-on. *She* shouldn't be because, well, there was still no future for them besides another night or three. Although, right now, the need for sex was almost enough.

Her lips parted beneath his, but there wasn't an ounce of submission in her. *Trap.* She lured him in via the best kind of sensual ambush, making a sound that was part delight, part moan. He threaded his fingers through her free hand, pinning her fingers above her head. Her hand closed around his in response, and he couldn't have broken free if he wanted to. Instead, he drank in the little sounds she made as her tongue twined with his, and they both fought to control the kiss and the heat. Kissing and kissing, because admitting defeat wasn't something either of them did.

"Tag—" She wriggled, her fingers and his loaner shirt trapped between them.

That was his name, he just had no idea what she meant. *Tag, kiss me some more?* Or, more likely, *Tag, back the hell up.*

"The bed's to your right. I'll take the couch."

Her lips parted, but no words came out. Her eyes got bigger, though, and he was staring at her mouth where her lips were swollen and pink from their kiss. He wanted to rub his thumb over their enticing plumpness, dip inside her there like lower, more southern parts of him wanted to do elsewhere. Except…she still wasn't saying anything, and this was likely why he didn't have a girlfriend, a live-in lover, or—God forbid—a fiancée like Daeg and Cal. They probably knew exactly what to say when their females stared back at them, all big, brown eyes. Maybe there was a user manual somewhere he could read up on, but right now he was on his own. And he had no damned idea what to say.

"Good night," he said and retreated to the living room.

MIA WASN'T MUCH for sleeping. Her head got too busy when she slept, and the nightmares were the least of her worries. At least those were over—more or less— when she woke up. Nope. Her real problem was *getting* to sleep. She'd been fine the first three months she'd been back, and then the problems had started. She woke up dozens of times a night, although she didn't always remember doing so. Sleeping pills didn't help, and, after trying them for a week, she'd abandoned any hopes of pharmaceutical assistance. The pills left her with cottonmouth and a sluggish, detached feeling nothing seemed to shake. She didn't need to be any more numb than she already was, so no, thanks. After her third wake-up call, she shoved herself upright and conceded defeat. Tag had a nice comfortable mattress with sheets that smelled like him. There was a neat stack of paperbacks on a bedside table, nonfiction bestsellers and a dog-eared copy of Sherlock Holmes stories. There wasn't much else in the room, though. Tag traveled light.

Lightning cracked overhead, followed by the low, echoing boom of thunder. The storms that had been rolling in all afternoon, dark purple streaks on the horizon, were finally there. Raindrops hit the French doors, tap-dancing on the glass.

She wasn't sure what she'd expected after the good-night kiss he'd given her, but sleeping alone hadn't been on her mental list. She hadn't expected a repeat of San Diego's hot sex—even if she'd been hoping—but the bed was a big one. The couch, on the other hand, was of the love seat variety. He couldn't possibly fit. She should check on him, make sure he was comfortable. Since she was up and all. She looked at her phone. Her cousin had noticed her absence and was predictably frantic. Since Mia couldn't teleport to the cruise ship, she settled for texting a few vague assurances that all was right in Mia land.

She padded out barefoot. As her eyes adjusted to the dark, her night vision kicked in. Everything was silvery gray, thanks to the moonlight pouring in. Given the miniscule size of the place, locating Tag was easy. He was, after all, the large, man-size shape sprawled on the tiny sofa, his legs hanging over one arm. He'd snagged a pillow from somewhere and then crashed hard, one arm slung over his head, the other resting on his stomach as his resident zoo supervised him. The ancient cat on the back of the sofa cracked one eye to glare at her, although the Chihuahua making itself at home between his legs didn't seem to mind her presence. Which was good, because staring at Tag asleep was something she could do for hours.

He looked sexy as hell, his chest bare where the throw blanket had dipped below the waistband of his sweatpants. Her pulse quickened as memories of their night together swept through her. She'd licked his taut abdomen, had teased her way down while he cursed and groaned and they both enjoyed themselves. All she had to do now was hook a finger in his sweats and tug, but… he also looked perfectly content where he was—and his couch was most definitely not built for two.

Her phone vibrated in her hand, and she looked down as a text from Laurel flashed across the screen.

Safe my ass. Where the hell are you?

In trouble.

She considered turning the phone off, but then her cousin would probably call out the National Guard—or, worse, Mia's brothers. Before she could second-guess herself, she snapped a cell-phone picture of Tag and sent it to her cousin.

Safe and sound. Catching up with an old friend.

There was a moment's silence and then:

Is he the hottie from the beach bar? He makes stranger danger look good.

How much to disclose?

You have to share.

Her cousin's next message followed fast on the heels of the last. A quick glance at the phone warned it was five in the morning.

Are you waking up—or just going to bed? Deflection was good.

I'm not the one who missed the boat.

She was never going to live her beach nap down. When her brothers found out, they'd hound her for years.

He offered me a place to stay for the night.

Hot sex had definitely *not* been part of the package. Is that code for dating? her cousin asked.

No. He's a Navy rescue swimmer who ships out in less than six weeks and who happens to have a spare couch.

Which *he* was sleeping on. Seconds later, her phone buzzed.

Typical. Email me more. Gotta catch some zzzz. Don't do anything I wouldn't do.

Unfortunately, Laurel's edict left plenty of ground uncovered. Mia's cousin had been a wild child before she'd met her husband-to-be. Picking up a hot-looking stranger on the beach was probably a misdemeanor in her cousin's book. Plus, all too reminiscent of Mia's own former fiancé, Tag was spectacularly unavailable for the long haul. So…her cousin had a point. Mia excelled at picking guys who were emotionally unavailable. Not that she'd done all that much picking, if she was being honest. She'd always *settled*.

Really, she hadn't been terribly surprised—or devastated—when her ex had made it clear he wouldn't be around when she was ready to get married. Or even get back stateside. He'd been a fun diversion, a good excuse not to look around. Because getting involved with someone—*really* involved—might mean letting someone get close. Giving up control.

Conveniently, Tag was another sailor who wasn't interested in settling down. They could have fun together while she considered what she wanted to do with her future. He was the perfect practice man. She slipped out of the room, cataloging the contents of the apartment as she went. Tag's place was probably really cute in the daylight, even if it was hard to imagine him picking it out. Someone had hung gauzy sheers over the window. The filmy fabric provided no real cover, but Mr. Bentley probably wasn't an enemy sniper, either.

When she heard the soft scrabbling noise coming from behind her, she almost dropped the phone. *Just a little noise. Nothing big, tall and deadly.* Whirling, she tracked the sound to a cardboard box beneath the front window. Adrenaline pumped through her, even as she knew, logically, there couldn't be anything bad hiding inside the box. It was just a box.

A box making thumping sounds.

Dropping to her knees, she peered inside. Five small black-and-white kittens ignored her intrusion and continued to wrestle.

"Can't sleep?" The raspy growl from the shadows behind her shot straight to her girly bits. Did he have any idea how sexy he sounded? The throw blanket hit the floor as he stood up.

"Occupational hazard." She tapped the side of the box. "You're stockpiling cats. Do these have names, too?"

"Occupational hazard," he said, and she could hear the grin in his voice as he mimicked her words. "They needed rescuing and I had a spare box. I haven't named them yet. You want to help?"

He'd given them more than four cardboard walls. The cats tumbled happily around inside, certain of their place in Tag's heart. He crouched down beside her as if a dark-o'clock rendezvous wasn't something out of the ordinary, reaching in to rub a small feline head, rough affection in each touch. The man was a mass of contradictions. He was a trained soldier and a dead accurate shot. He'd rappelled out of Blackhawks into some of the choppiest waters in the world, and, once there, he'd rescued some of Uncle Sam's finest—and plenty of other people. Her nipples tingled. And he loved cats.

The only things standing between herself and naked were his T-shirt and her bikini bottom. That wasn't a whole lot of clothing, even if her pink swimsuit wasn't exactly Agent Provocateur. Tag was deliciously, fabulously half-dressed himself. A pair of dark blue sweats hung low on his lean hips, revealing a stomach that was all delicious ridges and hard male planes.

She was staring.

Stop staring.

"Mia." There it was—her name in those growly tones again. Now she just had to have her way with him. Reaching out a hand, she traced the cut lines of his abdomen. How was she supposed to stay hands off when he looked like this?

"You're playing with fire."

She'd always been one of the boys. She loved her feminine side, but she was also an adrenaline junkie. Growing up as a younger sister with a host of older brothers and male cousins, it was either find some girls to play with—or keep up with the boys. She'd chosen option B but, when she was close to Tag like this, she felt impossibly female. They fit together somehow. Or maybe it was just sexual chemistry.

Honestly, she didn't really care.

"Come, play with me." Was that her voice, all low and throaty? She stood up and backed away, hoping he'd follow.

He took her up on her offer, his hands skimming up and down her back, the muscles in his thighs bunching as he walked her backward. She had a moment to wonder where he was taking her, then her back met the wall. *Naughty*. He held her there, or she let him pin her in place. It was all part of the same sexy package as he kissed her and kissed her, his fingers threading through hers.

Oh, yeah. An animal whuffled softly on the couch. *The boxer*, she thought through the haze of desire heating her up.

"Tell me you're feeling better." He leaned into her, staring into her eyes like he could read the answer there.

"*Make* me feel better."

"We shouldn't do this." He brushed his mouth over hers, though, so he couldn't possibly mean the words. Maybe it was a guy thing. Or a Tag thing. She really didn't care, not now when she ached to have his body on hers. In hers.

"It can be our secret," she said urgently, just in case he was feeling gun-shy. Or recalcitrant. Or anything else that would stop them from doing this. "No one has to know."

"Mia." Her name came out part laugh, part moan. He rested his forehead against hers.

"Are you as good as I remember?" The words flew out of her mouth, and, funny, she didn't want to take them back. She was actually okay with hooking up with him and letting the whole world know about it. This time, they weren't both serving in the military where the question of rank—and who outranked who—got in the way. This time, they were alone in his apartment and she was already half-dressed.

She wanted him. Badly. That was one secret she wouldn't be keeping. She wasn't sure who kissed who first, but Tag groaned, low and rough, his mouth devouring hers. His hands gripped her waist and she let him. Hell, her hands were all over him, too, dragging him toward her until she had his big, hard body flush with hers. He groaned again, so she hooked a finger into the waistband of his sweats and inched him closer.

Perfect. His erection was warm and hard, proof she wasn't alone in feeling this crazy, intense chemistry. Needing more, she pressed her front against his, rocking slowly, deliciously, against the thick ridge. His heart banged against his ribs, and she could feel each pounding note in her own chest. Having sex with Tag was insane, but he made her feel alive, and maybe that was the real reason she was climbing his big, beautiful body. She'd come too close to dying to *not* want to live now.

"How good are you at keeping secrets?"

She was the best. She'd kept secret the loneliness and the need. The desire for someone to connect with who would not only understand her but would love her. Tag wasn't offering love, but he was offering the next best thing. He was hot and sexy and, right now, perfectly happy for her to use him.

"I'm the best you'll ever have, so kiss me," she rasped, cupping his face between her hands and pulling his mouth back to hers. She didn't want words. She wanted action.

His bark of laughter was muffled by their kiss, but he seemed more than willing to oblige, she thought happily. He also didn't appear to mind her orders, although he seemed to interpret them his own way. He pushed a leg between hers, and a bright pulse of pleasure shot through her.

Wanting more, she wrapped a leg around his waist, savoring the intimate angle. When she ran her hands over his chest, his heart pounded beneath her fingertips, their ragged breathing all she heard. He fisted the hem of her T-shirt, the fabric bunching up in his grip as he pulled the cotton up.

The next moment, he was sliding down her body, taking her bikini bottom with him.

Play it safe.

Anticipation zinged through her, as if there was a direct connection between the panties he dragged down her legs and other places. His thumbs brushed the sensitive skin of her inner thighs. If they were having sex—reunion sex, fling sex, sex-up-against-a-wall sex—she was all in. Her bikini bottom hit the ground around her ankles, and she stepped out of it, toeing the fabric away.

Tag ran his fingers over her thighs. She had no idea how a rescue swimmer acquired such deliciously rough, callused fingertips, but she approved. Wholeheartedly.

"You sure about this?" He tipped his head back, so he could see her face. On his knees was a good look for him. Although she didn't make the mistake of thinking he was anything but in charge, no matter how much she pretended otherwise. His fingers pushed gently, firmly on her inner thigh.

"You going to make me wait all night?"

"Not a chance." His laugh ended with a groan. "Open for me."

Now *there* was a command she could get behind. She widened her stance, the wall pressing into her back and bare butt. Her new position should have been awkward, but instead it was intensely erotic, as if he couldn't wait long enough to take her to bed. As if he was every bit as impatient as she was.

He ran a finger over her center, where she was

wet and slick. *Oh.* She bit her lower lip. *So good.* She wanted, needed, another bright, hot jolt of pleasure. Threading her fingers through his short, dark hair, she urged him closer.

"Do it again. Don't stop."

He rubbed a thumb over her clit. *Yes. Touch me just like that.*

"We need to talk about this need you have for giving orders." She felt each word against her core, and she was going to kill him if he didn't stop talking and start *doing.* He touched her again, though, his thumb circling her until she dissolved in sensation, her breath coming in small, sharp huffs as the pleasure built.

He covered her with his mouth, his tongue replacing his thumb. His hands cupped her butt, supporting her as he pulled one leg over his shoulder.

"Hold on," he demanded.

She wasn't sure how she felt about the order—although she was fairly certain she'd regret her compliance later, much later—but she'd already lost control of the situation and it felt so good. And it was Tag after all. She grabbed his shoulders, doing as he'd demanded, because there was no holding back the tremors building deep inside her. He had to feel each spasm, her body clenching as she fought her way toward the orgasm she needed so badly.

She was still coming, the tiny after-spasms shaking her body, when he dropped her leg and went away. Then he was back, sliding on a condom before he lifted her butt and drove deep inside her. *Oh, yeah.* Fresh pleasure rocketed through her as he pinned her back against the wall.

"Wrap your legs around my waist."

He pulled out, pushed in again, thrusting deeper with each new, hard stroke. She quivered with each sweet invasion, but it wasn't enough, not quite.

"There. No. Higher." She covered his fingers with hers, moving him to *exactly* the right spot for her. Some things never changed. She buried her face in the crook of his neck, holding on to him. Breathing him in with each hard, sure stroke.

"Tag—"

"Right here with you," he growled against her throat. He moved faster, lifting her. Finding the perfect angle to drive her crazy. She rocked her hips against him, taking him deeper. His fingers pressed and twisted, finding the spot she liked so much, and she couldn't hold on any longer.

Dimly, she heard the boxer start barking up a storm as she came apart completely in Tag's arms. Mr. Bentley hollered something back, and none of it mattered. She dug her nails into Tag's beautiful, bare shoulders, his hands holding her up as he thrust and thrust again. The roof could come down or the door burst wide open. She didn't care.

"Jesus," he bit out. "You're—"

She didn't need to know how he would finish his sentence. She laid two fingers over his exquisite mouth.

"Take me to bed."

And, because his lips quirked up and they were still joined intimately, she added one more word, just to make him happy. "Please."

5

LIKE THE PAST 180 nights since she'd come home—or, more accurately, made it stateside—Mia jerked awake. Her head refused to let her body sleep uninterrupted because bad shit could be coming through the door. Or the window, the roof, or even the wall. She'd seen what a mortar round could do to plaster and rebar. Adrenaline hit her hard, her heart thumping erratically as she jackknifed upright. *Breathe.* In. Out. *Count.* Her fingers clenched the pillowcase. *One.* She was in bed. With Tag.

See? No enemy hostiles here. Everyone was friendly.

Breathe out. *Two.* His bedding smelled good, like Tide and dryer sheets. Had he picked the stuff out himself or had he just grabbed the first box he saw at the store? *Three.* At some point during the night, the sheet had tangled around her bare legs. The room was silent except for the soft in and out of the man breathing next to her. Breathing was good. Her brain skipped over that intel, not wanting to deal with the memories of other companions who hadn't been breathing.

Four. Her breathing leveled out. The room was empty of threats. See? She could lie back down like a

normal person and go to sleep. More breathing sounds
came from somewhere too close. A whuffling, snoring
sigh—a cat? Twisting, she spotted Tag's geriatric cat
curled up on the pillows between their heads like the
feline owned the place.

The Army psychologist she'd seen under much du-
ress had suggested counting. A little yoga breathing and
things would look better. Right. Tag's big, solid presence on the other side of the bed, on the other hand,
seemed to be her anchor in the semidarkness tonight.
She'd learned not to question what made her heartbeat
slow to a nice, steady pace. If it worked, good enough
for her. Interesting, though, how her head had decided
Tag was some kind of lifeline. Maybe it was the whole
rescue-swimmer thing. Maybe he gave off some kind
of white-knight vibe.

Or maybe it was just Tag.

She needed to move. The bedroom door was at her
five o'clock. Two windows lay at her nine o'clock. Unless a Stinger missile launcher blew a hole in Tag's
roof—unlikely—those were the only routes in and out
of the room. His room was clear. She slid out of bed silently and then checked the door and the windows. Just
to make certain. The courtyard was empty. Good. Part
of her had expected to find Mr. Bentley parked there,
ready to opine about what she and Tag had gotten up
to last night.

She blew out a breath as she scanned her surroundings one more time. Early morning light seeped into the
room. Apparently, Discovery Island actually had birds,
because they were making a ruckus outside. Apache.
Chinook. Black Hawk. Her bird identifying skills didn't
extend further than the standard Army fare. And roost-

ers. She could do roosters, too, but thankfully none of those appeared to be parked outside Tag's place. She moved around the bed and positioned herself where she could see Tag's wrist and his dive watch. It was six in the morning—civilized enough for her. Had she noticed how sexy his wrists were when she'd picked him up at the Star Bar? Because they *were*, strong and sprinkled with dark hairs. Even all relaxed as he slept, something about him read *powerful*. She had no idea why she was staring at his wrist, for crying out loud.

Okay, she knew. God. He was gorgeous.

Fall back.

They had some kind of weird power-struggle dynamic *thing* going on. The sexual tension between them was amazing and scary as hell at the same time. She really wasn't the kind of woman who did one-night stands, and yet Tag made her want to break those rules, again and again. He was her one and only exception.

She eyed her side of the bed. The sheets were probably cooling down, just the way she liked, and the pillow was punched down. *No.* See, that was what was wrong with this picture. She didn't have a *side of the bed*. She wasn't staying. He'd offered a place for the night. Nothing more.

It had to be her naked state making her think about hopping onto the bed and waking Tag up with a hand beneath the sheets. Morning sex was even better than good-night sex. *Stop it.* She needed her clothes. Before she could second-guess herself and get back in bed, she padded out into the hallway to recon where her stuff had ended up.

After all, since her luggage was currently headed to Mexico, she couldn't afford to lose the clothes she'd arrived with. Discovery Island didn't seem like the kind of place to have a Walmart. Fortunately, her clothes were exactly where she remembered parting company with them. More or less. They'd dropped her borrowed T-shirt on the living room floor, while her bikini bottoms were on the kitchen floor. Oh, boy. She had no idea how that had happened, although she had some mighty fine memories of Tag pressing her up against the wall and then working his way down... Yeah. He was the best cure ever for insomnia.

She took stock. Her assets at the moment consisted of a cell phone, a pair of shorts, a hoodie, two flip-flops, a T-shirt and twenty bucks. If she'd been former Spec Ops, she probably could have constructed an airplane out of the lot and flown back to the cruise ship. Since she wasn't, however, she'd need to come up with an alternative plan. For instance, she could phone her brothers and one of them would be here in half a day.

No. No how, no way.

She wasn't ten, and calling her family wasn't an option. Not only would she never live it down, she didn't *need* to. She had this situation under control. *As long as you stay out of Tag's bed*, a little voice whispered. *Because you don't have any control around* that *man*. Decision made, she bent over and grabbed the top.

"Do it again." Tag said, low and rough, from the shadows behind her.

MIA BENT OVER and naked in his living room was an excellent way to wake up. Far better than waking up alone and lined up on the left side of his bed, as if his head had been making room for her while he slept. And she'd stood him up. Whatever her reasons for abandoning the bedroom, the sound of his voice had her going all rigid. She turned around and there it was…the Mia glare he knew so well. Yeah, he was in trouble again, but it wasn't his fault she was all long legs and sun-kissed skin. Beneath the prickly exterior, she was real pretty, and what he'd seen when she reached down for her top ranked right up there in the category of world's sexiest sights. Her butt was all sweet curves and lower…

"So that's a no?" A man could hope.

"You shouldn't sneak up on me." She yanked the T-shirt over her head. Since she still had yesterday's swimsuit in her hands, she was naked underneath. Possibilities tempted him. He had the day off, and she'd already missed the boat. Literally. They could go back to bed together. He could think of plenty of things to do to pass the time until she was ready to figure out a game plan.

Was she blushing? He inspected her face more closely. Sure enough, a pink flush painted her cheeks.

"Are you embarrassed?" Imagining his take-charge master sergeant—emphasis on *master*—being self-conscious was a stretch, even if he did have an excellent imagination.

"I have a million things to do." The way she eyed his body—the *lower* half of his body—had him wondering what exactly was on her mental itinerary. Last night had been fantastic. She probably did have things to do, however. Things completely unrelated to his taking her back to bed. Mia always seemed to have a plan. She'd certainly organized yesterday's bridal group with frightening efficiency.

"For example?" He propped a shoulder against his kitchen wall and eyed the swimsuit in her hand. Mostly naked was a good start on his own personal agenda for the day.

"I need to call for new credit cards." She ticked her to-do's off on her fingers. "I need to let my cousin know my plans and make arrangements for my luggage to be forwarded from the cruise. Then I need to find the ferry schedule and book a hotel room until the cards can arrive. Is there a Western Union?"

She was almost out of fingers. "If you need money, I'm good for it."

Smooth, Johnson. Real smooth. She huffed out a breath. Did she think he was offering to pay her for last night? The idea rankled. Truth was, he'd make the offer of cash to any of his friends. She was in a tight spot and he could help. And...when had Sergeant Dominatrix become a friend? Or, rather, when had he developed friendly feelings toward her? Lust, absolutely. But friendship? A dangerous notion. "I'm happy to help," he said, meaning it.

She stared at him suspiciously, foot tapping. Somehow, she managed to look take-charge even though all she was wearing was his T-shirt. That shirt was his new favorite.

"I don't need a handout."

"Okay." He understood...because he'd feel the same way. And right now, he needed coffee. His head simply wasn't capable of getting into the game without a healthy dose of caffeine. He loaded up the Mr. Coffee, doubling the proportions. Scooping grounds he could do. Making the woman standing in his living room happy was a whole different proposition. Last night had been fantastic. Amazing. He had a feeling he was sporting a stupid grin. She, on the other hand, was making to-do lists.

Reaching up, he grabbed two mugs from the kitchen cupboard. His temporary place had come fully furnished, which meant he had a grand total of two mugs and two glasses. Two plates, two bowls and two sets of silverware. His kitchen was a veritable Noah's ark. At least they wouldn't have to share. Or drink straight from the pot, although he'd certainly done worse. For coffee, he had no reservations. He'd do whatever it took.

He shoved a mug in her direction. Bonus: whoever had picked the mugs had a sense of humor. His had Adam and Eve on the side. As soon as the two heated up, their fig leaves disappeared. It might be more than Mia wanted to see this early in the morning. "Cream and sugar?"

"Hit me," she said. "And don't hold back."

Huh. He wouldn't have guessed she had a sweet tooth. The sugar was buried under a stack of invoices and dive-supply catalogs. He nudged the pile out of the way, not entirely sure when his kitchen counter had become an adjunct office. Shoot. Compared to Mount Paperwork on Cal's desk, his stack was more steep hill than Alpine peak, but something had to change. Finding an office manager needed to be number one on *his* to-do list.

Maybe there was a solution to Mia's current dilemma they would both benefit from.

He narrowed his eyes at her. "How about a job, then?"

"You want to hire me? To do what?" Mia latched on to the mug, and he bit back a smile. She might not take handouts, but coffee was apparently an exception they had in common.

"The dive shop needs help." He pulled a carton of

coffee creamer out of the fridge. Damn it. He should go grocery shopping. He had three bottles of beer, the coffee creamer and a well-aged take-out container of hot-and-sour soup. Making her breakfast in bed was so not happening. Instead, he grabbed a few packets of sugar he'd boosted from the corner coffee shop and dropped them on the counter. She came around and reached for the creamer. His kitchen was approximately the size of a coffin, and her hip bumped his.

"Okay. You need more hands on deck. But again, where do I fit in?"

He couldn't tell if she was seriously considering his offer or not. Cal and Daeg wouldn't mind. They were swimming in paper when all of them preferred to be out on the water. They needed to be able to focus on what they did best: diving and rescuing. Mia could be a godsend.

"We need an office manager."

Humor lit her eyes. She took a sip from the mug, curling her hands around the side. "You want to play the boss and the secretary?"

Her mug was black with two rabbits on the front. As the hot coffee did its thing, the mug changed color. Purple with crazed bunnies replicating everywhere. *Yeah. He was subtle.*

She looked down at the mug. "Nice. I'm glad we used a condom."

The image of Mia holding a baby was shocking and unexpected. He had no idea where it came from or why it didn't have him running for the door. "I aim to please."

"You have good aim." She grinned at him.

"So, how about it? You want to come work with us?"

She was shaking her head almost before he got the question out. "I'm not planning on sticking around, but thanks. I'll call Visa and get them to send another card out here. I'll be out of your hair ASAP."

"Think about it. Even a temp until we can hire a full-time person would be helpful."

"We'd kill each other."

He gave her a bemused look. "I can restrain myself."

"Uh-huh."

Tag knew his concern wasn't something she wanted, but he worried about her. She was pretty much screwed, as far as he could tell. Her purse was somewhere between here and Mexico, and a job could help with her immediate cash flow problem. "You want breakfast? There's a breakfast burrito place near the dive shop—" Before he could finish the invitation, she was—as usual—two steps ahead of him.

"Go." She slapped a twenty-dollar bill into his hands. Damn it. He'd bet the bill represented all the cash she had on her at the moment. "Do the hunter-gatherer thing. Food sounds good."

Somehow, he found himself standing outside his own place. Shoes, check. Pants, check. Hell, he even had a shirt. Which was good, because even the burrito place had standards. He'd go this time because he hadn't missed the flash of vulnerability in her eyes—right now, she needed to be in charge. He was humoring her. Making sure she felt safe, because she was alone on his island and he owed her.

"Damn, boy." Mr. Bentley rolled his eyes, limping toward him. "She's got you coming and going, don't she?"

Also true.

"You want a burrito?"

TAG DISPOSED OF and breakfast arranged for, Mia kicked it into high gear. She sent a few quick Skype messages to her cousin, then arranged for new credit cards and an ATM card to be overnighted to her. At the twenty-minute mark, she'd booked a room at Sweet Moon's. Thank God for the power of PayPal and the internet. Okay, Tag had offered up his couch and his help, but she could do this without him. Unfortunately, her girly bits were all too happy to remind her of the areas where he *could* help.

She couldn't stop thinking about him, which was a problem. Hopefully one her Sweet Moon reservation would fix, because no matter how good last night had been, it was time to move on. She'd met more than her fair share of sailors, and she knew how this worked. He'd ship out. She'd stay behind or ship out in the opposite direction. Fantastic sex wouldn't lead to anything more and she was good with that.

Her stomach growled, reminding her that the calorie content of introspection was nonexistent. Just in case she'd misunderstood the state of Tag's refrigerator and squandered her last twenty dollars, she made a quick reconnaissance trip into his kitchen. Her search just confirmed her first impressions. The only food in the man's kitchen was for the four-legged residents, although even the kibble was starting to look like a possibility.

She and the Chihuahua were eyeing the bag when Tag arrived with a paper sack of breakfast burritos. He waved it in front of her, making her mouth water. He definitely had eggs and cilantro in there.

"You don't want to eat that."

"Not particularly," she said agreeably, now that people food was on the horizon. Before he could launch into twenty questions, she swiped the bag from him and dove in. Twenty bucks apparently went a long way on Discovery Island, or Tag had kicked in more. The bag yielded four tinfoil-wrapped, positively enormous burritos, along with a dozen little containers of green salsa and something suspiciously like refried beans. *Pass*.

"Is the Army coming over for breakfast, too?"

He shrugged. "You sounded hungry."

True. She hadn't realized he'd noticed.

"Someone's going to swing by later with some clothes for you to borrow," he continued.

"I can buy my own clothes." She didn't need a Tag-sponsored *Pretty Woman* moment. Plus, since she'd never seen the man in anything but T-shirts, she had her doubts about his abilities to moonlight as a stylist.

Another droll look from Tag. "Sure. If you want your wardrobe to consist of velvet sweatpants with rhinestones and flip-flops. Dani has better taste."

Okay. So he had a point there, but she didn't want to wear his girlfriend's stuff. *Oh, God. Did he have a girlfriend?* She mentally ran through the cheater's checklist she'd discovered in her latest issue of *Cosmopolitan*. He kept no girly stuff in the bathroom and she'd spotted no obvious signs of a female presence.

So screw it. She'd ask. "Who's Dani?"

"My partner's fiancée." He grinned at her. "He rescued her from a tropical storm we had a few months ago and she stuck around. Her grandparents run Sweet Moon's. Come on."

Grabbing their food and a fistful of paper napkins, he headed into the living room. Since he didn't own a dining room table, he tossed a few pillows onto the floor around a coffee table.

"Japanese style," he announced. "When the land-lord said the place was furnished, I didn't ask enough questions."

She picked a pillow, thinking he wouldn't have cared if all his rent bought him was four walls, a door and a bed.

"I've booked a cabin at Sweet Moon's, so I'll be out of your hair soon. FedEx should deliver my new cards on Tuesday."

"You don't have to leave. My sofa is your sofa."

She really, really did. It was a chivalrous offer, but they both knew where it would lead—right back to his big bed and the two of them going at it like sex-deprived maniacs. While she contemplated saying *yes, please!* to that particular fantasy, he leaned in and swiped her last salsa.

"Sweet Moon's seems perfectly lovely."

"I'm lovely." He rolled on to his back, balling up the wrapper and tossing it to the trash. Naturally, he made it. "Three point shot."

"Two. You had a straight shot at the basket, which is easier."

"I'd like to see you do better."

Of course he would. She'd always loved a challenge. Sitting up straighter, she took aim.

"Nuh-uh. From here." He patted the floor beside him. "It's only fair."

She could play by his rule. As she lined up her shot, however, he slid behind her and wrapped his big arms around her waist.

"You're not playing fair," she observed.

He brushed his mouth over her throat. "I'm using my resources."

"Is that what we're calling it?" Because she could come up with other words—like *seductive* and *sexy as hell*.

Her jaw flexed. She wasn't going to miss, no matter what he did. She'd dropped her Apache the equivalent of four stories once without interrupting the coordinates she was feeding back to the dispatcher. If she could do that, she could certainly handle one badly behaved rescue swimmer.

Except…he *reeeeeally* didn't play fair. He slid a hand up into her hair, pulling her ponytail free. The man had a fascination with her hair she just didn't get. His mouth, however, was busy doing things she really understood. Sexy, mouthwateringly good things.

Kisses.

Small kisses. Soft, sliding kisses that made her shiver in the best possible way as he covered the exposed curve of her neck with his mouth. Kisses that made concentrating seem a whole lot less fun than turning around and returning a few kisses of her own.

First, however, she needed to beat his ass at basketball. It was the principle of the thing. She settled back against him with a wiggle. If he wasn't playing fair, she didn't have to, either. His erection promised good times when they finished this little competition of theirs.

"Mia—"

She loved the growl in his voice. "Watch this."

The hand around her waist crept higher, his thumb brushing the underside of her breast. Lucky him—she hadn't worn a bra, since she was currently braless and luggageless. He knew it, too. He might have said something, but his words were lost against her skin.

She lobbed the bag into the open trash can, going for gold. "Four points for me."

"There's no four point shot in basketball." His thumb

moved higher, stroking gently over her nipple. Definitely a point for him.

"Three points for the shot, one for the distraction."

"You're the one who doesn't play fair." He sounded amused, not irritated. She probably deserved another bonus point for his good humor. She knew she was too take-charge, too fond of giving orders. Part of that was the military, but the rest of it was all her. "Next time, you should explain the rules before you get started." Turning, she slapped a hand against his chest and pushed him gently down. He didn't resist. Good man. The muscles in his abdomen flexed as he went, watching her face, a smile curving his mouth. Thank God for willing men.

She shouldn't do this but…she wanted to.

His back hit the floor, and he popped right up on his elbows. He was still wearing the smile—and far too many clothes. She needed to work on that.

"Are we done competing?" He smiled, a slow, lazy grin that crinkled the corners of his eyes and melted her insides. He was never in a rush, was just content to be in the moment and enjoy. In twenty or thirty years, when she was nothing more than a distant memory, he'd wear those smile lines on his face for everyone to see, and he'd be even more gorgeous than he was now.

She opted for honesty. "If you admit I won."

He gave a bark of laughter that ended abruptly when she scooted down his thighs, savoring the raw power of him between her legs. She was strong. She trained hard. They both knew, however, she couldn't hold him if he really wanted to get away. Not without hurting him and getting hurt in return.

"Mia—"

"You know what?" She ran a hand down his chest and the T-shirt with the Navy insignia on the front. "This offends me. Take it off."

He gave her The Look. The one that said he'd play any game she wanted, but it would be his turn to choose the next one. She could work with that. Muscles flexing and bunching, he pulled the shirt over his head and tossed it over his head toward the couch. His chest was a masterpiece, sun-kissed and cut. He still wore his dog tags, a visible reminder he was headed back to service and she wasn't. She had hers, but tucked away in a pocket of her duffel bag. The military part of her life was over.

"Better?" There it was—the rough growl she couldn't get enough of. Tag was so smooth and put together. She relished getting under his skin. Getting to *him*.

Oh. He had *no* idea.

"One night wasn't enough, was it?" he asked. Okay. She *might* have fantasized about having him again. Once or twice. A month.

"Not even close." He pressed his mouth against her throat and the pulse that told him exactly how she felt about him at the moment. They both wanted this, so why not?

She loved the feel of his thighs pressed beneath hers, all hard, rough power. Tag was a fighter and a soldier, but he also had a sweet side he hid from the world. He was *nice* in ways she absolutely wasn't. The man had an apartment full of rescued animals, for crying out loud.

And he'd added her to his collection.

She dragged her fingertips over his stomach and up his chest where his heart beat steady. When she hit the metal of his dog tags, she tugged lightly.

"You're sure you're not staying long-term on the island?"

"They're not a leash," he said dryly.

The heat that flashed through her was ridiculous. She needed a distraction because even though she knew there was no tying up—or tying down—a man like Tag, she had all these fantasies running through her head. So she slipped a finger beneath the band of his boxes, her fingertips bumping against the hot head of his erection.

"Hello." She grinned, popping the buttons on his jeans and doing some creative rearranging until she had him free and bare. She rubbed him with her palm, delighting in the way his head bumped demandingly against her hand.

"You like that," she said, as if she could tell him how to feel. Her skin felt too tight for her body, and she could hear her breathing picking up. Touching him turned her on. Lucky her. She stroked lightly up and down his shaft, taking her time because he felt so good and it had been a long time since she'd had this. Up, down, then back up again. Drawing small circles around the tip until the ragged sound of his breathing drowned out her own.

He pressed his thigh up, unerringly finding the place where she was hot and wet. For him. For her Navy man. Pleasure shuddered through her, and she froze. So good. So sweet and hot and absolutely what she needed right now. He cupped her jaw with his hand, urging her head up so he could see her face even as she curved her palm around him and rotated.

His eyes met hers in fierce demand. "I want a turn."

Of course he did. "You had one. Last night."

Her attraction to him was off the scale. For one moment, she panicked and considered beating a quick retreat. Because she was drawn to more than just his body. She liked the man himself. His teasing smile and easy good humor. He was tough as nails underneath the charm, but he didn't need to one-up or bulldoze over her. In fact, he didn't seem to mind when she took charge as long he got his turn.

"This is my reward," she whispered.

Moving down, she sucked the tip of him into her mouth. With a muttered curse, he shoved his jeans and boxers down. She helped because getting him naked was suddenly her first priority. He tasted salty and sweet. *Essence of Tag*, she thought, fighting back a smile as she ran her tongue over the swollen crown. She teased him, and he groaned, a harsh, needing sound.

Got you.

She kept her eyes open because she didn't want to miss a moment. This was worth waiting for, was a good reason to have spent all those years fighting to come home. Sunlight had started to fill up the room, and he really needed to buy some curtains that weren't sheer. She hoped like hell no one walked by in the next half hour or so. Giving Mr. Bentley a heart attack wasn't part of her master plan. She took more of Tag into her mouth, letting him push deeper. Licking and sucking every inch she could reach.

"I'd be happy to reciprocate." In response, she flicked a glance up at him. His face was strained, but his eyes were open, too. They had that much in common—they were both watchers. He threaded his fingers through her hair, stroking her shoulders, her arms. The little touches set her on fire. Rough-gentle and warm, the small caresses built the intimate connection between them.

She released him briefly, wrapping her fingers around him. "What are the odds someone walks by?"

While he calculated, she swept her hand up and down his shaft, her thumb and forefinger forming a tight O. She leaned forward and gave him a little lick.

"Pretty low." He tugged gingerly on her hair. "You could turn around. Give me something to do with my mouth. We could have our turns at the same time."

Imagine that. She could.

The problem was, she had no self-control around this man. Instead, she took him into her mouth again as deep as she could, until his head bumped lightly against the back of her throat.

Long minutes later, he tugged on her hair. Less carefully this time. She probably shouldn't find the little sting sexy.

She smiled up at him. Slowly. "You have something to say to me?"

Cosmopolitan had been right, she thought gleefully. His eyes darkened, and he looked like he was seconds from coming apart. God, she loved pleasuring him.

His grip on her hair relaxed, but the tension in his big body broadcast its own message. "I'm about done here. Am I coming in?"

Oh, please. She nodded, hoping like crazy he had a condom because the bedroom was too far away. He produced one from somewhere, foil tearing as he opened the packet and smoothed the rubber down.

She swung herself on top of him, positioning herself so the tip of him pressed against her opening. *Bull's-eye*. His hands gripped her hips, and he pushed up. She met his thrust, taking him deep inside her body until his balls were pressed against her.

"Okay?" he gritted out.

She didn't need a status check. She needed *more*. "Again."

"Bossy." But he complied.

She wrapped her legs around his hips, gripping him tightly. She needed more of this. He gave it to her, as if he knew without her saying anything or telling him how and where she needed his touch. He drove himself into her, and she could feel the control slipping away. His hips moved faster, harder, and she rode him, watching his face, fiercely focused on her and getting her where they both needed to go.

And she was getting left behind. Not that she minded so much. There was more to being here with him than just the sex—which was a dangerous thought. She filed it away for later because he moved his hand between them and found her.

"My turn."

He tapped her sweet spot, and she jerked, breaking the rhythm. He took over. One big hand curled around her hip, guiding her. The other flicked over her clit, pushing her higher. Giving her more and more. *Oh, please.*

"Now," he commanded. "Come for me now, Sergeant. I've got you, so you let go now."

She wanted to remind him she didn't take orders, not from him and certainly not here. But apparently she did. Air burst from her mouth in short, sharp pants as her whole world narrowed to this man and his fingers and his commands. He could see her face. No way she hid how he made her feel or just how out of control she was.

"Beautiful. You're beautiful." He petted her with his fingers, soothing her down as the spasms shuddered through her body. As his hips jerked against hers, his fingers gripping her close, part of her regretted the condom. She felt a primitive urge to have him mark her.

Or she could mark him. He wasn't in charge here, no matter how deliciously he claimed her.

"Not as beautiful as you," she said and she meant it. He was gorgeous. Big and hot and sweaty, he worked himself deep inside her body, thrusting in a rhythm guaranteed to drive her crazy. And, because she'd thought about marking him, she leaned up and bit his shoulder, just hard enough to leave an imprint. *Mine*.

"Uncalled for, Sergeant," he growled, but she didn't think he really minded because he let go then and so did she.

6

WHY WERE MONDAYS always such a bitch? The Bay-
liner was twenty-eight-feet long with two fishermen on
board. According to the owner's for-sale ad in the local
penny-saver, she had a 350 Chevy motor rebuilt from
scratch, new upholstery, six life jackets and a private
head. Right now, Tag figured the asking price was dropping fast, because what this particular boat didn't have
was a working pump. He hoped to God the two men on
board had been smart enough to wear the life jackets.

The steady roar of the rotors overhead made conversation difficult, so Tag leaned forward, bracing in
the open door. *There.* A white boat with blue pinstrip-
ing drifted on the ocean. Two men were on deck—
thankfully sporting bright orange life jackets—and
they immediately started signaling when they heard the
chopper. Raising his binoculars to his eyes, he examined the boat and the men for obvious signs of damage.

"We've got the *A One Anna Tuna* in our sights."

Cal flashed him a thumbs-up from the pilot's seat,
and Tag kept his eyes trained on the boat as they
banked and made a go-around pass. The recent storm

had kicked up the waters, and that translated into some pretty powerful waves. The *A One Anna Tuna* was too small to handle much in the way of a swell, and, although the men on board had tried valiantly to pump her out, she'd taken on water. The way she foundered as a new wave hit said she was in danger of rolling. And, just in case the rescue had seemed too easy, the *A One Anna Tuna* was also out of gas.

The plan was to drop a rescue swimmer on the hoist line with a replacement part. Just like playing Santa Claus, except they had water to contend with instead of snow. Easy-peasy.

On Daeg's signal, he braced himself into the open door with nothing between himself and the ocean but forty feet of open air. Good times. He launched himself out of the helicopter, head up and fins down. Seconds later, he punched through the water, kicking hard toward the fishing boat.

As soon as he was on deck, Cal and Daeg moved into position overheard, dropping the hoist line on his signal as the first crewman approached him.

"You all right?" The man looked tired but his color was good.

"Glad to see you and I'm looking forward to buying you a beer when we're all back on the island."

Yeah. He got that a lot in his line of work. He signaled Daeg to lower the cable. Metal flashed in the sunlight as his buddy hooked up the basket to the equipment ring and lowered the spare pump.

The basket descended from the chopper, landing dead center. He'd bet Daeg was a demon with those claw games, as well. He flashed Daeg a thumbs-up and waved off the fisherman when the guy moved in to help.

"Let the basket ground on the deck before we touch it." The helicopter's rotors could build up one hell of a charge. He didn't need to flirt with electrocution today. Fifteen minutes later, the *A One Anna Tuna* had a new temporary pump and enough in her tank to make it back to Discovery Island.

Tag rode the basket back up to the chopper, the empty gas can sitting pretty beside him. It felt like riding one of those fair rides, the litter swinging back and forth as the wind picked up, dotting the ocean surface below with little whitecaps, until Daeg pulled on the trail line, smoothing out the ride. Two minutes later, he was sliding inside the helicopter, and Daeg was breaking down the litter.

Cal's voice came on over the headset. "Is our *A One Anna Tuna* back in business?"

"Yes, mission complete." Tag shook his head wryly. The names people gave their boats never failed to amaze him. What was wrong with naming a boat something straightforward like *Bob*? He could have the *Bob I, Bob II,* maybe even a *Bob III* if the rescue business turned out to be a gold mine, or he was a really bad driver and burned through boats.

Daeg didn't share his enthusiasm when Tag voiced the thought. "You can't give a boat the kind of name you give your dog or your kid."

"Are you stockpiling baby names?"

Daeg didn't say anything, and that said it all, didn't it?

"*A One Anna Tuna* is pretty bad," Daeg finally admitted. "Thank God I've never been partial to *Anna* as a name."

"Gets stuck in your head, doesn't it?" He laid back

on the floor, watching the crazy swing of the sky outside the open bay.

"You bet."

Grinning, Daeg gave Tag a sly wink. "By the way, how's your weekend rescue doing? Did your Harley survive the sick up?"

"Five bucks it was too much tequila," Cal said over the radio.

Mia. "Beer's on you, then. It was motion sickness. She's a vet."

"One of those traumatic brain injury things?" That was classic Cal. Cut his leg off, and the man would swear he was okay. Tag didn't know who Mia had seen, but he didn't like the idea of her passing on a medical assist because of some misguided notion that real soldiers didn't ask for help.

He looked down at the ocean one more time, but the *A One Anna Tuna*'s crew had this. Plus, the Coast Guard was on their way to offer a tow if needed. He signaled Cal to head back to Discovery Island and dropped his head back onto the floor. Jesus. He needed a good night's sleep sometime this century.

"Yeah," he admitted. "She was Army and flew choppers."

"IED," Daeg said. "You've got the money shot right there. You drive over one of those, and, boom, it shakes your brain inside your Kevlar like a martini."

"Did you hook up with her friends?" Cal asked. "Take her to see Doc Evan?"

Discovery Island had an emergency clinic with a part-time doctor and a full-time nurse. The place kept business hours, though, and there had been nothing a doctor could do anyhow.

"She was alone." Because somehow an entire bridal party had failed to realize they'd left Mia behind.

Daeg turned his head and eyed him. "So…million dollar question. Where did you leave Hurling Beauty?"

"I took her home with me. Loaned her a shirt and a toothbrush."

"Jesus. Why'd you do that?" Cal's surprise came through loud and clear even over the headset.

Hello. "Because she was alone on a beach with most of her stuff on a cruise ship two hundred miles away?"

Daeg made a rude gesture. "Bring her to Sweet Moon's. Dani's grandparents can always use the business, and I guarantee it's not going to raise eyebrows."

He'd wanted her to stay at his place. Stupid, but there it was.

"Even I know you can't bring a total stranger to your place." Cal sounded irritated. "Even if she's not a slice-and-dice kind of gal, she's not going to feel comfortable spending the night with a random guy. Even if nothing's happening," he added hastily.

And…plenty had happened. "We're not strangers," he admitted. "We met in San Diego. We have some history."

History he was *not* sharing the details of.

"Where is she now?" Cal interrupted.

Daeg grinned. "Halfway to Mexico, if she's smart. Cabo's way more fun than Discovery Island."

"With me." He waited for the fallout.

Daeg shook his head. "You meet her on the beach and you take her home just like that?"

The chopper banked left in a lazy circle. Out of the open bay door, Tag could see Discovery Island growing closer. They'd be home soon.

"Tag—" Cal took them down nice and easy, heading for the landing zone. "You have to remember one thing."

"Hit me."

"She's not a cat."

"No. She's also not a dog, a rabbit or a guinea pig." He'd made the mistake of rescuing a tank of guinea pigs once. That was the same day he'd instituted a no-guinea-pig rule. The creatures were too similar to rodents for his taste, plus his cat had decided he'd brought home a snack. Yeah. Not a fun afternoon.

"You can't keep her. Not in a box, not at your place. You have to give her right back."

7

MIA SPOTTED THE house with its For Sale sign three miles into her five-mile Monday afternoon run. Since Tag had convinced her to cancel her Sweet Moon's reservation and stay with him for the remainder of her short stay on the island, she'd been enjoying her downtime. Discovery Island wasn't Cabo, but it had its charms.

And, thanks to that downtime, she had no problem slowing her pace and taking a closer look at the house. The summer cottage had a screened-in porch facing the ocean, peeling white paint and an overabundance of red-and-pink geraniums rather like lipstick on a slightly careworn woman. The color could have been a cheerful attempt at a fix-up or a general *screw you* to a critical universe, emotions Mia herself had felt too often. Her feet slowed even as her head nagged at her to pick up the pace. She wasn't staying, and she didn't need a house. FedEx would bring her new credit cards tomorrow, and then she'd head off-island. Problem solved.

As an officer, she'd been based in San Diego, but she'd spent most of her tours of duty overseas. She'd lived out of two duffel bags even when she'd been stateside, and none of the few rentals she'd stayed in had counted as a home. So if she'd flipped through freebie real estate brochures by the newspaper racks, that was her guilty secret. As was her desire to put down roots now that she was out of the military and her own woman.

It couldn't hurt to look, and the place seemed safe enough.

She hopped the fence, a waist-high formal white picket number almost swallowed up by a Leaning Tower of Pisa formed from delphiniums and tiger lilies. The simple fact she knew the names of the flowers only proved she'd been spending too much time with another new vice: gardening catalogs. It was amazing how many people wanted to sell her flower bulbs for a buck.

"You need a little love, don't you?" she asked the house as she picked her way toward the front porch. No one had mowed the lawn in about a hundred years, leading to more weeds than grass, but the weeds were beautiful. Sprays of bright yellow shot up everywhere, and a bushy red plant with rubbery leaves had gone to seed, spreading madly across the yard.

The house, of course, didn't answer her. Thank God. She didn't need to add *completely crazy* to her résumé. A gravel path led to a robin's-egg-blue front door with little stained glass panels. She crunched closer, noting the visible signs of rot in the sagging porch boards. Definitely a fixer-upper. That was okay. So was she.

Something moved underneath the porch. Sweat prickled her skin and not because of her run. She dropped to her knees, scanning the shadowy space half visible beneath the porch and the geranium screen. Two feet of space was more than large enough to accommodate a soldier. Or snakes, raccoons and a half-dozen other members of the animal kingdom. At least she could rule out sharks. *There*. The *something* twined against the geraniums, resolving into a flash of orange fur.

A cat.

Her house came with a cat.

"Hello, there," she crooned, inching closer just in case kitty was scared. Like a tiger crossed with a giraffe, the cat sported orange stripes on its sides and swirls going every which way. In addition to being colorful, the cat also came with a full quotient of feline confidence, as well, strolling out from underneath the porch like Mia's last commanding officer. It paused from a safe distance and looked at her, clearly waiting for something. Mia didn't have much experience with cats, but even she could tell that much.

"Yes, sir." The cat looked at her again in silent demand, chirped and disappeared back into the shadows. Right. She had her marching order. Gingerly, she stuck her head underneath the edge of the porch—she'd risk spiders for six inches and no farther—and realized kitty was definitely a girl. And hello…came with company. Five kittens blinked back at her from somebody's old T-shirt.

She fished out her cell from the pocket of her running shorts and called the number listed on the For Sale sign. The woman who answered was happy to send a Realtor out to show the place. Mia got the feeling the real estate market wasn't exactly booming on Discovery Island. The cat brushed against her bare leg. Whether kitty knew it or not, she needed a helping hand.

"I also need a cat rescued." She wasn't sure she was ready to take on a house *and* a family of five. She and kitty definitely needed to at least date first.

The woman on the other end of the line hesitated. Thinking things through, Mia hoped. "Discovery Island has a rescue team," she said finally.

"Good. Send them over." Mia repeated the address and hung up to wait.

Waiting wasn't her first choice. She'd done enough sitting around in the desert sandbox where she and her unit had been deployed. She was, however, good at it. She also knew a half-dozen different ways to get inside the house *without* the key, but she was turning over a new leaf. Pretending to be civilized and blessedly normal. Normal people definitely waited for the Realtor to come and let them in. Besides, on the off chance she wanted to put in a bid for the place, she didn't need to add one more item to the repair list.

TAG PARKED HIS truck in front of the run-down cottage. His Monday plans had not included getting called out to rescue a litter of kittens. On the other hand, since the search-and-rescue business was slow at the moment, there was no reason *not* to come. It was always good to be needed, and Mary Beth, the receptionist at the real estate agency, had sounded slightly frazzled. Plus, she'd promised him a cup of coffee for his efforts, so she had herself a double win right there.

"I can be had for two bucks worth of Joe," he said to Ben Franklin, who was riding shotgun. The dog barked happily in agreement as Tag got out of the truck and slammed the door. Since there were kittens to be recovered, the boxer needed to stay put for the moment. Afterward, Tag would make some introductions and test the possibilities.

And…triple win. The cottage also came with Mia.

Two days ago he'd offered her a job, and she'd thrown his offer back in his face. Shortly thereafter, she'd treated him to the best morning sex of his life and then organized a rapid departure for Sweet Moon's and some space of her own. He'd had to talk fast—and kiss plenty—to convince her to stay put with him. She didn't look now as if she had any regrets, either, although twenty-four hours probably wasn't enough time for her to entertain any regrets. Not that he wanted to find her starving in a ditch or beating her breast, but she looked perfectly happy. And impossibly sexy.

Jesus. He needed to get over this insane attraction he had to her. She wasn't his type, no matter how hot her running apparel was or how erotic his dreams last night had been. He'd bet she did yoga, too, because she stretched her leg on the porch railing, bending over in a way that did spectacular things for her butt in those skimpy shorts. She was definitely flexible. She had on one of those bra tops that managed to hold everything in place in a feat of engineering he thoroughly applauded. Sweat beaded her skin, slicked the sun-kissed valley between her breasts. He wanted to devour her from head to foot. *No.* He was here on a job.

"You're in so much trouble here, soldier," he muttered to himself, and then he deliberately brought his boot down hard on the path. She was jumpy as hell; he didn't need to scare her.

Her head shot up, and she twisted around, glaring at him. An orange tabby cat wreathed around her ankles, and he'd bet the damned thing was purring. He would be if she let him close. She frowned and opened her mouth.

"Search and rescue," he said, before she could say anything. "I'm here in my official capacity."

"They sent you?" To his eternal disappointment, she dropped her leg. He'd been admiring the view.

"Discovery Island doesn't have Animal Control," he said lightly. "I'm the best they've got."

She exhaled, blowing her hair off her face. "Right. And sending a Navy search-and-rescue swimmer didn't seem like overkill for six felines?"

Something else he didn't bother answering. Instead, he looked down at the cat marking her leg possessively. Again, an urge he completely understood. "That's one. Where are cats two through six?"

She smiled slowly. Yeah. He was in trouble. "Under the porch," she said and pointed, while Ben Franklin barked encouragement from the truck.

This was why he preferred water. Sure, the ocean was well-stocked with predators and a good storm surge could beat the hell out of a swimmer, but those waters were also spiderless. And he had a mask and a wetsuit.

"Damn," he sighed.

"Have at it," she said, sounding amused. Apparently, her help didn't extend past making a phone call for a rescue assist, because she dropped down onto the step to watch him work. He made a quick detour back to his truck and grabbed a pet carrier and a can of tuna fish from the bed. He wasn't above bribery.

Momma cat was happy to accept the treat. Unfortunately, she was the only one. He flashed Mia a smile and then dropped on to his stomach and started crawling. It was just like boot camp, except no one shouted obscenities and urged him to go faster.

"Are you looking at this place?" Sure enough, the porch's underside was liberally festooned with cobwebs and where there were cobwebs…yeah. *Not* thinking about eight-legged surprises was probably his wisest move. Two feet in, he spied his target, an ancient T-shirt swaddling a handful of kittens.

He set the tuna-fish can down, but the kittens didn't budge. Maybe momma had trained them not to accept candy from strangers.

"Excuse me?" Mia's voice floated down from the porch. She was smart enough to stay far, far away from the glorious kingdom of spiders.

"Talk to me," he ordered, inching forward slowly. If the kittens bolted, he'd have to go under the house and the odds of his getting stuck would go up exponentially. He made a note to add a smaller person to their search-and-rescue team ASAP. "If I'm braving spiders to rescue your kittens, the least you can do is talk to me."

"They're not mine." He didn't miss the note of uncertainty in her voice.

"Finders, keepers," he muttered and tugged gently on the T-shirt. After all, as she knew very well, *he* had a menagerie and a half at his place, so where else would the kittens go but home with them? The island wasn't big enough to have an animal shelter. "I'm going to hand them out to you, and you're going to put them in the carrier, okay?"

The porch creaked as Mia stood up, so he decided she was on board with his plan. The first four kittens didn't object too strenuously when he plucked them out of their nest and carefully handed them over to Mia. Kitten number five, however, didn't think any amount of tuna fish could compensate for the indignity of being removed from its bed. It beelined for the back wall. Damn it. He lunged and… *Got you.*

"Did you lose one? I can't have a kitten lost under my house."

"*Your* house?" He handed over the escapee kitten by executing a strategic tuck and roll onto his back. Their fingers brushed as he handed over his prize. She didn't react, just competently tucked the kitten into the crowded carrier.

"It's for sale," she said defensively. "Maybe I want to buy it."

House lust, not man lust. That put him in his place. Her reasons for sticking around on Discovery Island didn't include him. He had no idea where the notion had come from, but he scuttled it fast. He'd obviously been around Daeg and Cal too long. Possibly, diamond rings and happily-ever-afters were contagious.

"Is staying with me that bad?" As far as he knew, she'd been planning on leaving the island some day in the very near future. The question was rude, but he didn't care. Mia understood *blunt*. Frankly, anything else was lost on her.

"Eager to be rid of me?" She sounded unconcerned. She also clearly had no intention of sharing her long-term plans with him, but he was good at guessing. The military recommended at least thirty days of downtime before former soldiers tried to reintegrate, find a job and all that crap. Mia would take whatever time she needed to get her feet on the ground and her head straight. And whatever plans she made were her business. He was deploying soon, so what did it matter to him?

He gently shook the T-shirt-nest, just to make sure he'd gotten everyone. No man left behind, even if the *man* in question had four legs and a tail and weighed less than two pounds.

His instincts must have been talking up a storm be-cause…bonus kitten. The first five kittens matched, but the sixth was a white-and-orange Siamese that stuck out like a sore thumb. There had been some two daddy action here.

"Momma here apparently had herself a ménage." The last kitten was feistier than her brothers and sis-ters, too. Hissing and spitting, it sprinted, tail up, ears back, for the crawl space under the house. Damn it. He *hated* small spaces.

A CAR CRUNCHED to a stop in front of the cottage to the accompaniment of Ben Franklin's happy, excited bark. The older model BMW screamed *posh* and *drive me fast*. A woman who had to be the Realtor popped the driver's-side door, swung her legs out and froze. Mia followed the other woman's gaze…straight to Tag's mighty fine butt sticking out from under the porch. The man was definitely worth a second glance. Her own eyes certainly refused to stop looking. She'd had him twice yesterday, and she was no closer to being over him than before. Their sexual chemistry was off the charts.

The possessiveness welling up in her was less familiar—or understandable. She didn't have any claim on Tag, but apparently her brain hadn't fully processed the message. Viewing the house suddenly seemed less important than keeping the Realtor far, far away from Tag. Just in case he was in a dating mood.

The real estate agent pulled herself together and tapped up the path toward Mia, smile in place and hand extended.

"I'm Mary Jane Barker. M.J." She eyed Tag's butt again, seemingly not put off by the loud cursing emanating from under the porch. The last kitten was apparently posing a challenge. Whatever. If Tag could handle a South Pacific tsunami, he could certainly take charge of one small feline.

M.J. sported a chic little pantsuit number and espadrilles. She'd come prepared for business, too, with an enormous tote bag and an iPad. While Tag chased the last kitten, Mia explained her interest in the place. Casual-like, of course.

The agent was all uh-huh-uh-huh, but clearly distracted while she fished in the bottomless bag for a flyer. Mia eyeballed the numbers on the four-color ad while the Realtor finished ogling Tag, who was now backing out, an orange-and-white kitten cupped against his broad chest. He'd had more than one close encounter with the dirt and leaves from the jasmine strangling the porch's decorative trim. A particularly large leaf was stuck on his very fine butt. *Bonus.*

"You look like you could use a hand." The Realtor's throaty purr had Mia biting her tongue. Really? She wanted to buy a house and all the agent could do was flirt with Tag? Oblivious to Mia, the other woman leaned in and brushed random bits of vegetation out of Tag's hair as she worked up her nerve to go for the gold and remove the leaf from Tag's butt.

Mia could see where this was going. The Realtor would manufacture a constant stream of endangered animals so she could call on Tag to come out and help her. She'd probably produce a rhinoceros or a ten-foot crocodile next. Tag's apartment was already full up with rescues. Cats, dogs, the mangy rabbit and…her.

Apparently, however, Tag had defensive moves of his own. He took a step backward, bumping up against

Mia, and her hormones revved in approval. He was big and male and...leafy.

"Honey," he said, and she didn't think he was discussing bee-based toast products. Large hands curled around her shoulders, and his mouth brushed her throat. Her nipples tightened immediately which was probably all too obvious to everyone, thanks to her sports bra. God, did he have any clue what he was doing to her...? The Realtor stared first at Tag and then switched her gaze to Mia. Yeah. That made two of them who were confused. Maybe Tag had hit his head under there.

"Are the two of you a couple?"

And just like that...she was getting ideas.

"He's poaching on your preserve," someone—an *old* someone from the sounds of the voice—yelled from the direction of the BMW.

THE VOICE BELLOWING from the car was horribly familiar. *Shit.* Not only had Mia managed to call the one real estate agent on the island whom Tag would really like to avoid...but the Realtor had brought along her grandmother and Tag's nemesis.

Ever since he'd rescued her from her fender bender with the ocean, Ellie Damiano had been determined to pair Tag with M.J.

Loudly determined.

There was absolutely, positively nothing wrong with M.J. She was attractive, well-educated and employed. He'd bet she had a 401K and dental insurance and, if he'd been even remotely interested in settling down, he would have gone out with her. She wasn't the kind of woman a man had casual sex with, though, and he wasn't the kind of guy who settled down. In approximately six weeks, he'd be getting his ass shot at, and there was always a chance he wouldn't be coming home. Wherever that was. So, for once in his dating life, he was going to do the right thing and steer clear of long-term women.

M.J., however, hadn't received that particular memo. She was confident, smart and could manage logistics with the deftness of a four-star general. *She* thought Tag should expand his dating horizons and go out with her while he was on the island. She was apparently fine with the whole deployment thing, as well, although she'd also made it clear that she'd be working on changing his mind.

He should just say *yes*.

Have a couple of drinks.

Kiss the woman and test for chemistry.

Except…he kind of already knew the answer. M.J. was a stunning woman, but he didn't click with her like he did with Mia. For some reason—and he really had a beef to pick with the universe about this one—all he had to do was be near her, and his body went up in flames. His imagination went crazy, imagining all the wicked possibilities of his tongue on her skin, her mouth, her…

Yeah.

He and Mia had chemistry.

He and M.J.? Not so much.

"Get in there and fight for your man," Ellie bellowed from the car.

"Sorry." M.J. made a face. "I brought Grandma Ellie. Her aide had the afternoon off and I can't leave her by herself."

No. She couldn't. The last time she'd left her grandmother alone, Ellie Damiano had hot-wired the car and taken it to the store to stock up on picnic supplies for a romantic evening out with a beau. Tag still wasn't sure whether or not the boyfriend was imaginary—and he did *not* want to know since said picnic supplies included a tube of flavored lube and a disposable bullet vibrator—but M.J.'s grandmother had driven the car off the road and into the ocean. Fortunately, the water hadn't been deep, but she'd wrecked the undercarriage. Tag had waded in, calmed her down, carried her to shore… and been stuck with her ever since.

He really needed to choose his rescues more carefully.

Ellie rolled the BMW's window all the way down. "I'm doing you a favor, boy. It's a Robin Hood thing. You saved my life. Now I get to stick by your side until I've saved yours. M.J. downloaded it on Netflix for me so I could see."

Moving to a technology-free community suddenly seemed a whole lot more attractive. Was it too late to become Amish?

"You don't owe me anything, Mrs. Damiano."

Let alone your granddaughter. *Please.*

He looked over at M.J., who had the decency to look embarrassed. "I don't suppose you have those child-safety lock things?"

M.J. shook her head and then smiled. "You buy this house and I'll upgrade the car."

M.J. was more like her grandmother than he'd realized.

Ellie leaned out the car window. Another few inches and he'd be looking at rescue number two. "She's pretty. You're pretty. I'll have the best-looking grandkids on the island."

There was no possible response, so he stayed silent.

"You take your time," Ellie hollered back. "Check out the bedrooms. I'll just be here taking a little nap and picking out baby names."

Was Mia enjoying the show? He was pretty sure she was, because she wasn't the object of crazy granny's matchmaking schemes. But since she really deserved an explanation—if only because she'd managed to keep a straight face during all this—he gave her one. "I rescued Mrs. Damiano. Now she wants to pay me back."

"IN FLESH," MUTTERED M.J., sounding disgruntled. Apparently, the other woman wasn't a fan of the barter system after all. "Are you two dating? A girlfriend would certainly shut her up."

Mia had no idea how to explain her relationship with Tag. Apparently, she didn't need to, however, because Tag beat her to the punch.

"You bet," he said, and then his mouth met her neck again in a move guaranteed to make her melt. Which was wrong. She didn't *melt*. She was frozen and distant. Closed off. Whatever. Her ex had tossed plenty of adjectives her way when she'd returned, and some of them were even true. Letting people get too close was a mistake when you were playing in the sandbox. People died. They didn't come back. On Monday, six of you sat down to argue hockey scores or compare fantasy teams and eat. On Tuesday, you could be five. "Mia and I are absolutely dating. In fact, we're engaged. I'm completely off the market, and you can tell your grandmother so."

Tag's voice came out all low and husky. He also wrapped his arms around her waist and squeezed. She had no idea why he'd just announced their engagement, but parts of him were clearly ready to skip straight to the honeymoon. She wriggled a little against the thick ridge pushing against her butt because he deserved to suffer, too.

"A little help here? Mrs. Damiano is a force of nature." He muttered a rough plea against her ear. Then he *nipped*. The bright spark of pleasure was one good reason to humor him. Plus, having Tag at her mercy was a fantasy she particularly enjoyed.

"Baby," she cooed, taking the Siamese from him. "I thought this was our little secret?"

Tag floundering had to be the cutest thing ever. Her big, gruff sailor was afraid of what she'd say next. So what the hell? *He* needed *her* help, and she was supposed to be practicing her new normal, right? She'd wanted a man and a family, a regular job and the mortgage and white picket fence to go with it.

She handed the kitten to the Realtor, stood up on tiptoe, flinging her arms around his neck and whispering, "You didn't tell me this was in the job description."

She'd had her way with him yesterday, but he'd handed her a second opportunity. Hooking a finger in his dog tags, she yanked him closer, feeling the silent laughter shake his chest. Laughter and Tag went together like sun and a day at the beach. He made her feel happy, made her want to smile.

He also made her hot as hell.

All good things.

His body hit hers with just a little extra oomph that had to be deliberate. And as his legs brushed hers, his front pressed right where she wanted him. He knew what he did to her. His dark eyes gleamed down at her, still laughing and right there in the moment with her.

"Bad boy," she said throatily.

"Are you complaining?" He cradled her hips with his hands, his thumbs rubbing small circles that were part tickle, part pleasure. He hadn't left an inch of space between them, which made it clear he shared her interest because she could feel every delicious inch of his erection. She wrapped his tags around her fingers, pulling his head down to hers. Oh, look, she had a Navy rescue swimmer on her own personal chain. How perfect was that? She slid her other arm up his and cupped the back of his neck.

His mouth hovered an inch above hers. "Is this where I kiss you to shut you up? Or to seal the deal?"

She grinned because his words sure didn't sound like a complaint. "Sounds like a plan."

"Choices." She felt rather than saw his smile as his lips covered hers. He gave her a perfectly well-behaved public kiss—except for what their lower bodies were doing—but the kiss wasn't enough. She wanted him misbehaving, so she nipped his lower lip, demanding *more*. He took over, his tongue parting her lips and sweeping inside her mouth. A little rough, a whole lot sexy.

Tag Johnson didn't have a tame bone in his body as his sweet, lazy, take-charge kiss proved. Because that's what he did—take charge of her. His mouth devoured hers, sending the hot pleasure streaking through hers. Swept off her feet, she got a stranglehold on his dog tags because letting go now was impossible, even if he made her knees go weak. He kissed her and kissed her, as hungry for the contact as she was.

His hands pinned her in place against him. Her nipples tingled as heat swirled through her. Oh, he was good. *Thank God.* She'd come back from Afghanistan, determined to live, to enjoy every moment she had. For the soldiers she hadn't been able to bring back, for the women she'd met there who lived lives she couldn't begin to comprehend. For *herself.* So she kissed him back, her tongue tangling with his. Meeting his stroke for stroke. Around him, she was out of control and she *liked* it.

Behind them, M.J. coughed. "I'll just open up the house. You two come on in when you're ready."

So much for keeping this thing between them under wraps and their own wicked secret. He'd announced their engagement, and then they'd kissed, and if there weren't pictures on the island's Facebook page within the hour, she'd be shocked. And, clearly, not much shocked her these days. Otherwise, she wouldn't have kissed the daylights out of this man in front of an audience.

She pulled away from their steamy lip-lock with a sigh of regret. They really, really couldn't have sex on the front porch, and buying the cottage was only the first hurdle to that particular fantasy. Heat and need darkened his eyes, and his breathing was every bit as ragged as hers. Still, he'd apparently rediscovered his responsible side, because he captured her wrists and gently tugged her hands down.

"Behave," he ordered. "We can't do this."

She hoped that was an unspoken *here* she heard, because he drove her crazy, and he couldn't kiss her like that and not make good on all his unspoken promises. Half a weekend with Tag had been nowhere near enough time.

"It takes two." And he definitely wasn't helping. With a husky groan, he brushed his mouth over hers one more time in a quick, hard kiss, and then he let her go.

"Let's check out your house," he said and headed for the door. That left her staring at his butt, so she made herself useful and plucked the leaf off his back pocket.

"Mia." Her name came out part mutter, part laugh. And she liked it, liked knowing he had no idea what to do with her. Other than the obvious, of course. If she careened out of control around him, well, he was in the same boat.

She handed him the leaf. "You're collecting souvenirs, sailor."

"Shoot. If I'm wearing spiders, you're removing those, too."

"You're on your own there." Then she gave into temptation. Her hand landed on his leafless butt in a gentle smack. His eyes widened, as if he couldn't quite believe she'd done that. That was fun, but she had a house calling her name. It was safer if she removed her hands from Tag's too-tempting body and confined her inspection to the rooms. She'd bet the place had a bedroom or two. If he wanted to play fiancé, she could be convinced to let him. Still, she couldn't resist getting in the last word as she brushed past him into the cottage.

"When you mentioned *keeping secrets*, I didn't know this was what you had in mind."

HOLY. WOW.

Mia brushed past him into the house, even though there was plenty of room for her to avoid the full body contact. She was clearly making a point of her own with that possessive little smack. He grinned. He'd return that particular favor at the soonest, most public opportunity possible. She was full of surprises today. He had no idea why she was jonesing to look at houses, but whatever.

Then, because some things had to be said, he hollered the words after her.

"Taking your nickname to new levels, Sergeant Dominatrix?"

After all, he'd just crawled butt-first in front of the woman wearing leaves on his ass. He'd abandoned all claims to dignity somewhere around the point where he'd kissed her holding a kitten *and* wearing vegetation.

She paused, her foot on the bottom stair.

This would be good. He shouldn't tease her, because the name wasn't nice, and nicknames could be cruel. Still, she was the one who had smacked his ass. She had some responsibility here. The only question was: Did she have a sense of humor hiding under her crusty exterior?

"You didn't want to play house?"

He heard the words come out of her mouth, but nothing about them computed. He had a bad feeling he blinked at her like a fish out of water.

"Mommy and Daddy? Doctor? No, wait." She made a face. "We haven't done that one yet. Later."

Yeah. Like he had a frame of reference for that. He'd been one of *those boys* growing up, the kind who was a magnet for trouble. He'd created makeshift swords and lances from whatever he found. Sticks, the cardboard tubes from the Christmas wrapping paper—anything long and remotely straight. Duct tape had been his best friend, and he'd spent hours feinting and parrying. Since the window had closed on being a medieval warrior—unless he hauled his butt out to Vegas and joined the dinner show circuit at Excalibur—and there weren't any job openings for ninjas, either, he'd decided when he was twelve that he would become a

Marine. Or a Navy SEAL. A Green Beret. Israeli Special Forces. His twelve-year-old self had been fuzzy on national identity, but long on fighting for a good cause.

"Is that what we were doing?"

"Hey, *you* proposed to *me*. I was just getting into the spirit of things."

"You smacked my butt," he growled, because he couldn't think about actually being married to this woman right now. He should have explained to her that he'd blurted out an excuse, that there was nothing real about their engagement except…it didn't feel fake. It felt right.

"Baby, just wait until tonight." Her grin lit up her face. "I expect you to come bearing gifts." She waggled her ring finger at him. Ah, yes. He'd just called her his fiancée in front of the island's biggest gossip. There was no chance in hell the Realtor wasn't tweeting her big scoop from one of the upstairs bedrooms. If he was lucky, she hadn't snapped a picture of their kiss.

Mia turned and disappeared into what had once been the dining room. The only recognizable part of its former eatery status was a dust-wreathed chandelier dripping those diamond-like crystal thingies. It was certainly sparkly, tossing sunlight around the room. As far as he was concerned, it was just a room, but Mia wandered in with a look of rapture on her face. A look pretty damn close to the one she wore when she came for him. Imagine that. He'd been put in his place by a chandelier.

Time to check on his rescues. He fell back to the front porch and the cat carrier, whose occupants were happily taking a nap. Scooping out a kitten, he lifted the squirming bundle. Definitely a boy and a kindred soul. "We're in so much trouble here, buddy."

With typical feline indifference, the kitten mewed and wriggled, wanting down or possibly even teleportation out of his hand and back under the porch. Damned if he knew what it wanted, which also seemed to be his usual state of affairs around Mia. The kitten he could fix. He popped it into the carrier with its companions.

Announcing their engagement had been an impulse. He had no idea where those words had come from, but he'd better do some damage control.

Need to give you a heads up, he texted Cal. He'd be seeing the other man soon, but texting seemed simpler than face-to-face conversation.

Hit me.

He could imagine Cal kicked back on the boat or in his own fixer-upper house he was so in love with. The man relished knocking down walls and rehabbing.

I just asked Mia Brandt to marry me.

Okay. So he'd told her. There had been absolutely no asking involved. If they'd been genuinely engaged, she'd have held it over his head for the next fifty years or so, and he wouldn't have blamed her.

Cal's next text was short and pithy: Wow.

Yeah. That, too. The thing was, Mia was more than a convenient coconspirator. Sure, she was a good sport about his surprise announcement, and sleeping with her was flat-out incredible. In fact, if he was being honest with himself, Mia herself was pretty incredible. She was tough and funny, and he loved the way she was determined to live her life.

Fast work. You sure about this?

Yep. He'd pretty much lost his mind.
Sure? Not in a million years.
In it for the long haul? That wasn't him.
He'd also never looked for the easy out before. Becoming a rescue swimmer hadn't been a walk in the park. He'd had to try twice before he'd succeeded. Some men got it in one; others tried three and four times and still didn't make it to the end of the course. While he hadn't rung out, he'd failed. So he'd picked himself up and tried again.

Piper wants to know if you set a date. And if you got down on one knee.

Hell no. It's a fake engagement Gets M.J.'s granny off my back, he texted back. He felt the grin tug at his mouth. Getting down on his knees in front of Mia would be a mistake. She might be bossy and stubborn, but she also got to him in ways he couldn't explain. It wasn't just her sexy outside—although he definitely loved looking at her. Nope. It was something about the woman inside. Of course, she also spouted orders better than any drill sergeant he'd ever had, and that was a problem because he didn't do orders. Or edicts, suggestions or direct commands.

And, if they both needed to be in charge, he didn't know where that left them.

8

An hour later, Mia was officially in love. The cottage was absolutely perfect, other than a few minor cosmetic issues. And a desperate need for a new roof. On a scale of one to ten, where *one* was move-in ready and *ten* was a total tear-down, the cottage scored closer to ten than she liked, but the place was worth it. It felt…right.

She turned to the Realtor. "Can you give us a few minutes alone?"

M.J. beamed, clearly scenting blood in the water. Or her six and a half percent commission. "Sure," she said. "Flip the lock on your way out and take all the time you want. When you're ready to make an offer, you've got my card. I could start the paperwork now even, and then you could swing by later this afternoon and sign it. Just give me a *yes*."

As soon as Mia had landed stateside after her last tour, she'd shipped right back out. She was the last person who knew anything about sticking. About permanency. And yet she knew she wanted *this*. This cottage. This life in this place.

"It seems to be my day to say *yes*." She elbowed Tag, and he grunted.

M.J. left with a chipper wave, stopping to coo at the kittens in their carrier. Apparently, she wasn't able to resist all the furry cuteness. Mia felt marginally better about her own momentary weakness.

She pointed to the departing agent. "You've got new home number one right there, if you close the sale."

"I'm not worried about the kittens. M.J. will definitely take one, and I'll find homes for the rest." He stamped on the floor in front of the fireplace. "The wood's soft here."

She eyed the spot he was pointing to, but it looked normal enough. The hardwood was a warm honey color, streaked and pitted with all the living that had happened in the cottage. Leaded glass fronted the bookcases flanking the fireplace, and a big picture window looked out toward the ocean. Despite the gazillion trees between the house and the water, she could just spot a sliver of blue. She'd get two armchairs and put them right there. She didn't need two chairs, seeing as how she was a party of one, but it would look nice. She could sit and stare at the waves. Almost.

"You really want to make an offer on this place?" He poked a windowsill, and his finger sank through the soft, pliant wood.

She really did, although admitting the truth out loud seemed like a guaranteed jinx. Instead, she went for the deflection. "What's up with this engagement of ours?"

"Surprised you, huh?

She arched a brow. They both knew he hadn't genuinely meant what he'd said. And it didn't matter if a little flicker of happiness had shot through her thinking about the two of them as a long-term couple. It was just he'd hit on her weakness. She wanted a normal relationship, one *not* broken up by tours of duty and temporary base housing.

"I—" He scrubbed a hand over his head, clearly at a loss for words.

Yeah. She'd bet it was hard explaining why you'd announced your engagement to a near-stranger without asking the fiancée first.

"Just tell me," she suggested. "Don't try to dress it up. I'm hard to offend."

"It's just that everyone on the island has been trying to fix me up since I got here. It gets old fast, saying *no* all the time."

"Poor baby, all those women chasing you."

He looked offended. "That didn't come out right. Yes, there were women."

"Did they bring you casseroles?"

"What? No." He grinned. "Although hot dishes could have been nice."

"Now I know the way to your heart," she teased. "Bring food. But your dating woes don't explain our engagement."

"Cal and Daeg know the truth. They also know what a pain in the butt Mrs. Damiano is. Hell, the whole island wants to fix me up."

"Let me introduce you to a phrase—*just say no*."

He leaned back against the wall, arms folded over his chest. "I tried. I ended up with two dates in a week—and there aren't even *that* many women on the island."

Tag's problem was that he was too *nice* to say no. Fortunately for him, *she* wasn't nice at all. In fact, she'd made being a bitch a bit of a specialty. "Not a marrying man?"

"I'm Navy. I ship out. Leaving doesn't seem like a good foundation for a long-term partnership."

"So I'm a red herring." She'd been worse, done worse.

"You're a miracle worker." He nodded at the real estate flyer she held. "Although I thought you were leaving. Instead, you're contemplating becoming a real estate maven."

"Plans change." Not hers, ever. She'd always had a six-month plan—plus a two-year, five-year and ten-year plan. The simple fact, though, was that she was here on Discovery Island and strangely planless. The minute the cruise ship had sailed, her itinerary had flown out the window. It should have been scary as hell. Instead, it was liberating.

He hesitated. "Do you want me to set M.J. straight?"

Being engaged to Tag was normal, right? Kind of a dry run for whenever she did meet the guy of her dreams and settle down for good. Practice couldn't hurt, because, yeah, her social skills were beyond rusty. Plus...

"Are you going to put out?"

He didn't respond, just gave her the crooked grin that tugged on her insides. She'd borrow him, she decided. He was out of here soon anyway.

"Fine. Okay. I'll be your loaner fiancée for the next six weeks or so."

A halo of sunshine poured in the window, lighting him up. Tag Johnson was no saint, however, and they both knew it.

He took a step toward her, and she honestly had no

idea if he planned to hug her. Kiss her. Shake her hand. Anything was a possibility. "Thank you," he said.

He did, however, have mighty fine manners.

"Be careful. Now I can sue you for breach of promise." She winked at him and moved into the kitchen. A new coat of white paint and the room would be gorgeous. Afternoon light flooded over the subway tile on the floor and lit up the little crystal knobs on the cupboards.

"I appreciate your restraint," he said dryly on her heels. "You ever live in a small town?"

"If base counts, I'll go with *yes*."

He thought about her words for a moment. "Soldiers gossip. I'll give you that."

"Tattle, complain, whine, bitch and share far too much," she agreed. "You can take your pick. I swear, my unit was better than Twitter. M.J. seems like she's cut from the same cloth. All of Discovery Island is going to hear about our engagement by tonight."

"Or sooner. Last chance to head her off at the pass. Are you truly okay with it?"

Surprisingly, yes, she was.

9

THREE DAYS AFTER making an offer on the cottage, Mia tapped the Call End button on her phone, the less-than-happy news from her mortgage broker ringing in her ears. If Mother Nature had been playing along, there would be sound effects. Thunder and lightning or perhaps—if her life was a movie—the *Jaws* theme song playing in the background. Instead, all she got was another perfect day on Discovery Island.

Perfect weather-wise, at least.

Since her house buying had hit a definite snag, she wasn't in the mood to admire the sky or lie out on the beach.

If she wanted a loan, she needed a job. She got that. On the other hand, she had cash in the bank, enough to cover the modest price of the cottage. Not wanting to burn through it all, however, she'd planned on funding half the cottage and then using the rest of her savings for much-needed repairs. Her mortgage broker had other ideas. So she either bought a fixer-upper and then did no fixing, or…she found a job.

Working wasn't the problem. She was fairly certain Tag had meant his offer of employment, and she was desperate enough to do some arm-twisting if she had to. Unfortunately, Tag was more likely to demand other things from her. Things involving words like *begging* and *groveling*. She would have, if she'd been in his place. So she had a plan—she just didn't like it.

She eyed Deep Dive, but Tag's place looked like your typical dive shop and not one of the seven circles of hell. It was a few minutes past noon, and the morning divers had just returned, hauling their tanks up from the boat and washing out wet suits and gear in the tank in front of the shop. Their post-dive wrap-up managed to be both cheerful and loud. Even lurking on the sidewalk, she could hear divers swapping *Did you see the...* stories as they one-upped each other with fish tales.

Highly *suspect* fish tales. Mia was fairly certain the guy closest to her had not, in fact, spotted a twenty-foot hammerhead shark. Asking for help sucked. She'd rather be wrangling the hammerhead.

As if he could read her mind, Tag popped the door open and stuck his head out. His hair was damp as if he'd just stepped out of the shower, a scenario she could imagine all too easily. The slow, knowing smile he gave her made her want to scream. He couldn't possibly know her mortgage broker. She'd called someone off-island, and it wasn't like she was wearing a sign reading Desperate Woman Here.

"Are you coming in?" He waggled his fingers at her. "Or are you planning on standing there all day?"

As if it hadn't been three days since he'd announced their pseudo-engagement and she'd kissed him. Okay. She'd practically scaled his big, tempting body on the front porch of what she really, really hoped was her new house. *Details.*

"Baby." Since two could play at this game, she gave him a saccharine sweet grin and followed him inside. She needed to talk to him—*beg*, the little voice in her head noted—and an audience wasn't her first choice, so inside it was. He disappeared through a side door and…wow. The command center Tag and his boys had set up here would have made Uncle Sam proud. Floor-to-ceiling monitors displayed real-time information about weather conditions, and banks of high-powered computers filled the available floor space. A radar map tracked incoming weather. The sun outside explained the calm inside, but Mia could imagine what happened when a storm hit.

Tag dropped down onto a chair, swung his feet up onto the desk, and leaned back. Nope. He had no intention of making this easy for her.

"Coffee?" He pointed to an ancient Mr. Coffee as low-tech as the rest of the room was high-tech. She weighed her need for caffeine against the sludge-like consistency of the liquid in the pot, and her stomach voted *no*.

"Uh…I'm good."

Or would be, as soon she got this over with.

He shrugged, clearly in no hurry. Of course, he wasn't the one who needed an insta-job and wanted to get it wrapped before five o'clock, to boot. It was just Tag, she reminded herself. She recognized the old dive-shop T-shirt he wore—which said something about the state of either his wardrobe or his washing machine—and his military cargo pants and steel-toes were famil-iar gear. He looked badass and sexy as hell, which of course made her want to swing herself onto his lap and ride him like a cowgirl. Kiss him some and see if she could distract him from his work. Which, a quick eyeball of the room revealed, they had all to themselves. Given the amount of high-dollar hardware in here, the door had to have at least one lock.

She could have the place locked down in less than a minute and then…

No. House first.

Then sex? Her libido begged.

"Tag, I—" Her voice cracked, the throaty rasp giving her away.

She moved toward him, not sure how to start. Getting her hands on his body, however, would probably send the wrong message. Deceptively simple lines of text covered his computer screen. She'd bet the code was as elegant and lean as the man lounging in front of the screen. He could probably blow up the world with a few keystrokes.

"So." His eyes gleamed as he pressed a combination of keys and blanked his screen. Tag had always been good at giving her his undivided attention. "To what do I owe the honor of this visit?"

Stalling sounded good to her. "You don't need to watch the screen?"

"In case there's a killer storm barreling up the Pacific I've been blissfully unaware of for the last three days?" His amused smile shouldn't have made her panties wet. "We're good. I've got all the time in the world for you."

Oh, damn. Where did she start?

"Three guesses," she said huskily. When she perched on the edge of his desk, he didn't even blink. Of course, the surface was also preternaturally clear. No stacks of papers or binders for her butt to crush or knock over. He probably figured he was okay.

"You came to say *hello* to your fiancé." He folded his

arms over his chest and grinned at her. He had a really nice chest. She should have looked at him and seen a threat. Instead, she saw safety. How strange.

"Nice try. Do your boys know?"

"That we're engaged? Absolutely. That you're just using me for my body? That, too." He leaned forward and clasped her hand. He gently dug his thumbs into her palm, massaging away the tension there. She might marry him for real if he'd just promise to do the same every night.

"You came to check your kitten. I'm holding him for you until you've got your new place." He nodded toward the cardboard box tucked underneath his desk.

Rescuing things—people, military missions, felines— apparently came second nature to the man. She, on the other hand, wasn't nice. She'd served and she'd fought hard, but this time she was getting what she wanted. Still, she had a feeling she wouldn't be leaving empty-handed.

"You know you want to." A teasing smile flashed across his face. Problem number one? She didn't even *want* to resist Tag. When he reached down and lifted the orange-and-white Siamese out of the box, she was lost.

"You don't fight fair."

"I saved you the best one," he said. "The others have already been promised. You can thank me later. Here."

With no choice but to take the kitten, she cupped her hands and let Tag place the Siamese in her palms. The kitten tumbled into a small heap and then started giving her thumb a bath, industriously running its rough sandpaper tongue over her skin. Maybe it liked her. Or maybe it was leftover chicken salad from lunch making her so attractive.

She needed to get back on solid ground. "I could be persuaded."

"How?" He swiveled in his chair, his shoulder bumping her thigh. While he waited for her answer, he reached down and plucked out a second kitten. The small bundle of warm and wriggly was accompanied by a motorboat-size purr. It looked fragile, but anything living under that porch had to have a core of steel.

Tag watched her kitten for a moment. "He needs you."

"Or he's hungry."

She liked the idea of being needed, though. Serving in the military, she'd had a job to do and a place on the team. Her teammates had needed her to perform, and she had. Now that she was done serving, however, she wasn't sure what to do next.

"Do I win a prize?" he drawled.

"For…?"

"For being right about why you came. I'm hoping it involves sexual favors."

She shook her head. "That's not why I came."

"Huh." He ran a finger down her thigh. When Dani had dropped off an armload of loaner clothes, Mia had registered the lack of practical, everyday stuff. Dani's clothes were feminine. Flirty and fun. All things Mia wasn't. Case in point? Her sundress. The skirt was yellow with tiny white polka dots. It was cheerful as hell and not something she would ever have bought. But since she felt different here on this island, why *not* wear it? "It's not my charming good looks, is it?"

"I need a job." She blurted the words out. *Smooth.* She'd practiced what she was going to say, but apparently her brain had abandoned the script. "I want that job you mentioned, if it's still available."

He raised a brow. Shit. He was going to make her work for this, wasn't he? "I believe your exact words were *over my dead body.*"

"Not true. I asked you if you had ambitions to play boss and secretary, and then I declined to participate." She pointed to his kitten. "Fur baby there is about to take a header off your desk."

Effortlessly, he rerouted the kitten. Too bad it wasn't as easy for the two-legged folks in the room to do the same.

He curled his fingers around her kitten, stroking. The sensual jolt that went through her had to be coincidence. "So, Sam here doesn't interest you?"

She really, really wished he didn't, but too late. Tag had made it clear this was *her* kitten, and that she was keeping it. God, she hoped not. She had enough males in her life, thank you very much.

"I said I'd changed my mind."

"Cat. Job. Next thing you know, you'll be setting a date." He shook his head in mock dismay.

"Are you going to hire me or not?" She gritted the words out. Why did he have to make this so hard?

His finger traced a wicked return path back up her thigh, the fabric of her borrowed sundress rucking up beneath his touch. It was just a finger. She shouldn't be thinking about jumping his bones right here in his command center. Or how easy it would be for him to nudge her skirt out of the way.

"Is it a conflict of interest if I hire my own fiancée?"

"Better than someone else's. Plus, I'm good. You wanted an office manager."

"I wanted a temp to help with the paperwork."

She leaned in. "I'm better than a temp. We both know it."

"You're so certain?"

Yes, yes she was.

"You're bossy. You're take-charge." He ticked her attributes off on his fingers.

"I'm good at what I do." She carefully set the kitten back on the desk. "Do you want me to beg? Because I can probably manage it. I'm going to have to draw the line at groveling, though."

A grin split his handsome face. "Hell, yeah. Begging works for me. But I'll settle for you saying: 'Tag, I need your help.'"

"You don't want a *pretty please with sugar on top* to go with it?"

"Mia…" He made a *give it up* gesture. "You have to say it. Give me that much."

Fine. She could do this. Think of the house. "I need your help. Please."

The words ran together, and the last word wasn't as audible as the first but…she'd done it. And he rewarded her with a quick, hard kiss.

"My pleasure."

No. It was *her* pleasure.

MIA CLUTCHED SAM, looking slightly dazed. Good, because that made two of them. He didn't know what he was doing here, either, although he definitely recognized the feeling flooding through him. Satisfaction. Maybe his prickly ex-sergeant needed him for something more than sex.

"Why the sudden interest in the job now?"

"I want the house I saw." A fiercely possessive tone shot through her voice and made him wonder: What would it take to make her talk about him the same way?

She was still talking, though, so he forced his attention back to the here and now. "The mortgage broker wants me to have gainful employment before the bank commits to funding me. Hire me." She paused a moment, then added, "Please."

Yanking open a desk drawer, he rifled through an explosion of paper and produced a W2. "Fill this out and we'll get you on the payroll. Your desk is over there."

She followed his gaze and sucked in a breath. "I don't think you're paying me enough."

"You don't know how much I'm paying you."

"It can't possibly be enough." She shook her head as if she'd never seen a mountain of papers hiding a desk before. True, the entire surface was covered, but they needed help. He'd made his position perfectly clear.

"Give me the job description."

She held out a hand, as if he'd actually bothered to write a bullet-point list when he was drowning in paper.

"Dream on," he said, fighting the urge to grab her hand and pull. One good tug and he could have her laid out on top of the paper she'd stink-eyed. He might even consider clearing her desk for her with one good shove and *then* following her down for some illicit one-on-one. There were plenty of wicked things he could do to her. With her.

"Earth to Tag." She tapped his shoulder. "Unless you're paying me to stand around while you daydream. In which case, lucky me. This is going to be a sinecure."

Right. Job duties. "Bottom line is whatever Deep Dive needs. Right now, that's someone to coordinate our rescue-training ops and the first-responder team. There's also going to be a mountain of paperwork." He grinned at her. "Literally. We also book adventure dives, and we're doing a Train Like Spec Ops program with Fiesta cruise lines."

She didn't look fazed. "What kind of rescues do you get called out to?"

"Drifting boats, foundered boats, missing fishermen, crashes, storm survivors."

"So basically when a boat goes ass up, literally or metaphorically, you're the rescue party."

Her description worked for him. "You bet. Here's the thing. Whatever we choose to do outside of the office, when we're *in* the office, I'm in charge. I run the ship and you take orders. I need to know you can accept that."

She looked at him, her face not giving anything away. He told himself he didn't care if she was ticked off or not. They needed to get some things clear, and who was running the show at Deep Dive was one of them. Because while they'd been lovers and he'd like to think he knew something about her, he wasn't kidding himself. Mia had plenty of secrets. Saying she liked to be in charge was an understatement, because she was bossy as hell. And honestly, he didn't mind when they were in bed. He had plenty of demands of his own, and as long as everybody had a good time, he was fine. When they were in the workplace…well, all bets were off. His world. His rules.

"You're blunt," she said finally.

"We're not colleagues, and search and rescue can't be a democracy. Sometimes, someone has to give the orders and someone else has to follow. I'm your boss."

She looked at him for a long moment.

"Right." He'd never heard a woman sound so unconvinced. "How medieval of you. So I'm the one taking orders. Okay."

"Okay?" Somehow, he'd expected resistance from her. Mia absolutely loved being the one in control.

"Okay, but only in the office. Anywhere else, orders are off-limits."

Her gaze was one hundred percent challenge. Just as he was brainstorming a dozen different ways to show her exactly who was in charge here, Daeg joined them, schlepping an oversize gear bag. He wore a bright red T-shirt sporting an *I love my accountant* message and a goofy grin that had Tag wondering if the loving in question was a recent occurrence.

The man was a lost cause. "Nice shirt."

Daeg patted his chest. "Now you're just jealous."

"Dream on, buddy."

Daeg looked over at Mia who, having reorganized the papers on her new desk into three equidistant piles, now had her head bent over the W2, printing her information in neat block letters.

"Is it bring-your-girl to work day? I didn't get a memo."

"Meet Mia, our new office manager."

He made the introductions, and Daeg grinned at him. "So this is Mia, the mystery fiancée. Congratulations on the engagement of convenience. May the island gossips remain blissfully ignorant."

MIA WASN'T SURE how she felt about the alliterative name, but it seemed like a nice first. She'd never been a woman of mystery before. Since her previous roles had been as the buddy and the boss, this was a welcome change.

Apparently done teasing her, Tag grabbed Daeg and

the two of them settled around a large conference table with a large box of green plastic soldiers. Not playing, she quickly realized, but sketching out the beginnings of a disaster-recovery training exercise Deep Dive would be leading in the coming month.

She also met Cal, the founding member of Deep Dive, as well, but he was quickly sucked into the training preparations. The rumble of male voices filled the command center as they pushed the figures around, comparing various scenarios. Planning also seemed to require a great deal of good-natured arguing about the relative merits of the different scenarios.

While the guys plotted world domination or super-hero rescues—the two seemed suspiciously similar— she organized the office filing system and sorted bills. She also made lists of necessary office supplies. Some-how, it was no surprise to discover the guys had a FEMA-worthy collection of emergency provisions and a gazillion dollars worth of computer hardware, but no staples or butterfly clips. She'd bet if she checked the office fridge, she'd find energy drinks and bottled water, but no coffee creamer.

Mia was happily lost in creating to-do lists when the door slammed open, and an attractive woman came barreling in. Of average height, she had a great body and honey-colored hair. Based on the T-shirt alone, the woman had to be Daeg's fiancée, which meant, thank God, she was taken. Her pink shirt announced *I'm the accountant your mother warned you about.*

Tag shoved to his feet. "We just got our cue to leave."

Dani threw her arms around Daeg's neck, pulling his head down to hers. *Too late.* With all the kissing not three feet from her, Mia was getting ideas of her own.

Wow. Good thing she had a practice fiancé of her own or she might have been envious. "It's like working in a love nest. I assume you've explained the definition of *sexual harassment* to them both?"

A smile tugged at the corner of Tag's mouth. "Fortunately for Daeg, he's not paying Dani."

She let Tag tug her to feet, curious to see what he would do next. "Horrific, isn't it? We have to hire family now or we'd get sued for sexual harassment on a weekly basis. You don't want to see what comes next. We'll go grab some lunch. Hopefully, when we come back, they'll have cleared out. Or finished."

Daeg flipped him the bird, but he didn't leave off kissing his fiancée—and apparently all the PDA wasn't contagious. Tag didn't kiss her. Of course, she didn't want him to. They were in the office, for God's sake. His hands-off behavior wasn't disappointing at all.

Not in the slightest.

"What if I do? Want to see what comes next?" Shoot. Her question sounded either creepily close to the marriage ceremony or outright pervy.

"You're full of surprises." He sounded…approving?

Whatever. Since he was clearly waiting for her to make a move—and, equally clearly, Dani and Daeg weren't wrapping up their marathon kissing session anytime soon—she reached under her desk for her bag.

"Come on," he said. "We'll hit the taco truck, and then I'll take you to get the stuff you'll need for Sam when the two of you move into your new house."

_10_

THE DEEP DIVE team spent the night searching for a missing fishing charter, which was a hell of a way to kick off the weekend. Three overdue boaters had been reported as missing to the Coast Guard by their families. Although there was no distress call, the fishermen had been due back to Discovery Island by six o'clock, and now, twelve hours later, there still hadn't been so much as a peep from the absent men.

Looking for the twenty-seven-foot _Fish Me Crazy_ visually was like looking for a needle in a haystack. Radar showed nothing within a twenty-mile radius of Discovery Island, and the Coast Guard's urgent marine broadcast to other boaters had turned up no leads. Before the Coast Guard launched a jet, they'd reached out to Deep Dive to send up a rescue helicopter.

The sun had just cracked the horizon, turning everything shades of gray. It was Tag's favorite time of day to fly, the ocean calm and peaceful on a good day, and nothing had ended badly yet because the day was young. Deep Dive had put up a team of four—one pilot, two swimmers and one hoist operator—and Tag would be first into the water if the job required it. Mentally, he divided the blue water up into quadrants, scanning one before moving on to the next. Sunlight glinted off the surface. With a decent ceiling and plenty of visibility, he was feeling good about this particular mission.

"Operations normal." The familiar words of Cal reporting in to the Coast Guard base back on the mainland washed over him. They'd make the call every fifteen minutes until they found the missing fishermen or had to turn back because they were running low on fuel.

Thirty miles out from Discovery Island, he spotted debris in the water. Cal banked, bringing the chopper around and down until they hovered low enough over the water for a visual. What had looked like fiberglass hull from several hundred feet in the air turned out to be a semi-submerged piece of lumber and a small flotilla of plastic bottles. *Not* the *Fish Me Crazy* or pieces of her. Those were the rescues that sucked, when the mission became salvage, and there was nothing he could do but pick up the pieces and bring them back. Maybe it helped the people left behind to know what had happened. Closure and *blah blah blah*. He'd take survivors any day.

From the chopper, the ocean looked like one big expanse of blue, the surface broken by the occasional whitecap or shadow of a larger fish or shark passing by. Seagulls crisscrossed the sky because they weren't so far from land, only seventy miles or so. Cal read off the gas levels over the headphones. They had another hour before they'd have to turn back to refuel.

Ten minutes later, they came up on the *Fish Me Crazy*. She'd flipped and was floating keel up. A quick head count, however, turned up three heads. Although the crew had gone into the water, they'd managed to don life jackets first and were now clinging to the boat. As the team drew nearer, two of the men in the water signaled for help, waving their arms over their heads.

While Cal radioed in the boat's position and the presence of three survivors in the water with life jackets, Tag dropped a marine location marker to record the survivors' current position in the ocean. Losing sight of the men down there could be fatal. Fortunately, there didn't appear to be any fuel in the water.

"Bull's-eye." Daeg high-fived him as the flare hit the water, gushing white smoke and yellow flame.

While Cal radioed for a Coast Guard patrol boat to assist with a possible tow, Daeg and Tag assessed the weather conditions. Although the wind was running almost twenty knots per hour, the waves remained a relatively modest six feet. Sure, the ocean below was no swimming pool, but Tag had swum in far worse. The reasons why the *Fish Me Crazy* had rolled weren't immediately clear, however. Rogue wave? Poor maneuverability? There was no way to know. "We're going to put them in the swing and hoist them up." Cal stared at him steadily. "As quick as we can, because they've been in the water for a while and they're going to be tired."

"Got it." Pulling on the rescue strop, he connected the tending line to the V ring on his harness and then moved into the ready position in the door. Cal steadied him, a hand hooked in the harness, while Ben kept the chopper nice and stable, the wash from the rotors pushing out the water. After one final safety check on his gear, he stepped out, and Cal lowered him down.

Arms crossed over his chest, fins down, he entered the water. Swimming free of the rescue strop, he stroked hard through the explosion of bubbles around his face, aiming for the surface and the boat. A quick visual check for hazards turned up nothing—the surface was clear and pretty aside from the rotor wash from the helicopter. Any debris from the *Fish Me Crazy* was long gone. Looking up, he signaled he was okay. *Another fine day at the office.*

Getting his head above water, he swam toward the survivors. They looked pretty good for guys who'd spent the night in the water. The one closest to him was pale and clearly fatigued, though, so Tag made a quick decision to send him up first. Reversing, he stopped six feet out. No signs of panic. Good. The last thing he needed today was someone trying to climb him like a ladder.

"You brought the cavalry." The guy on the end flashed him a thumbs-up, clearly ready to get out of the ocean and back home. Tag didn't blame him.

He spat out his snorkel. "Better. I've brought you some US Navy boys. I need you to turn around and show me your back. Then I'm going to take you one at a time to the sling. Next, it's an easy ride up to the chopper. You first."

He pointed toward the pale guy, who nodded.

"Happy to go," he said. "Just tell me what to do…"

"Turn around and let me do all the heavy lifting." As soon as he had a clear shot of the guy's back, he grabbed the life jacket and kicked. The man planed out, floating on his back with feet pointing up, and they headed to the pickup point and the rescue litter. After securing the man, Tag grabbed the line and steadied the basket as it rose. The guy's day wouldn't be improved by banging into the side of the chopper. Then it was rinse and repeat with the other two.

"If you're done down there, we'll head for home."

Cal's voice came on over his radio, sounding satisfied, as he should. This rescue had been textbook perfect. While Tag didn't mind a little adrenaline rush, nice and easy wasn't a bad thing, either. The three fishermen undoubtedly agreed.

The line descended from the chopper and he swam over to the hoist, connecting his strop to the rescue hook and signaling for pickup. When he rose up out of the water, he shoved his mask back. The ocean looked like a blue-and-white curved ball from his perch, deceptively calm as the *Fish Me Crazy*'s crew now knew. Daeg braced a booted foot against the chopper bay as he reached out to steady the hoist and bring Tag in, safe and sound. They were all going home, which made today a damned perfect day.

Mia had promised to "make him dinner at his place" later tonight which was code for "pick up takeout." If he was lucky, it was also code for "waiting naked on the kitchen counter." Probably not, but he liked the fantasy. Having a female someone waiting for him was different, although he shouldn't get used to it. Still, although he'd go back to San Diego and she'd stay here, he had every intention of enjoying tonight. The twelve or so hours until then promised to crawl.

Daeg slapped his back as the chopper turned around and flew toward the island. "Bet you're going to miss all this excitement when you head back to San Diego."

Tag rolled his eyes. "Yeah, right." Uncle Sam's job description included plenty of high adrenaline jobs, including jungle and coastline extractions. And since the op called for breaking up a drug-running ring, there would undoubtedly be plenty of bullets and do-or-die moments. The South American coastline, particularly near Brazil, was also well known for its shark attacks.

Yet somehow, it didn't seem as…*something* as before.

It was no contest that serving in the Navy was exciting work, plus it made a difference. He didn't kid himself about that. Sure, he knew the three guys they'd just pulled from the water cared a whole hell of a lot about today's rescue, as did their families, but in the end, they were just a handful of people. Heading down to South America, Tag had a chance to take a real blow at the drug trade. He'd be bringing home soldiers, and he'd be taking out part of a drug pipeline destroying tens of thousands of families right here in his own country.

And yet he couldn't stop thinking about Mia settling down here in her cottage with Sam, the orange-and-white cat. Putting down all sorts of permanent roots. He couldn't imagine himself doing the same. Okay. Apparently he was doing so now, but it was an aberration. As soon as his boots hit the tarmac in San Diego, he'd remember exactly why he'd signed up for another mission. Staying put on Discovery Island was just a fun little fantasy.

Nothing serious.

MIA'S OFFICIAL WORK hours were flexible, but she liked starting the day at dark o'clock. She also liked being at the dive shop before things really got hopping. The search-and-rescue piece was more scintillating—when it didn't involve crawling around under porches rescuing kittens—but early morning on Discovery Island was pretty. Since the dive shop was located on the boardwalk, she had an ocean view from the "office." The marina was surprisingly busy, with commercial fishing boats and charters headed out for a day of deep-sea fishing, while divers hauled tanks and weights to waiting dive boats. The sense of excitement and going places appealed to her.

Tag had texted her last night that they'd been called out on a rescue job, so she was on her own this morning until they made it back. No worries. She had it handled. She popped open the folding sign announcing the special of the day—a particularly challenging site where the divers often spotted sharks—and placed it on the sidewalk. The nearby dive shop had a chalkboard with fancy curlicue writing and colored chalk. Meanwhile, Deep Dive…had a whiteboard, a black marker and block lettering.

Houston, we have a problem.

Or chalkboard envy.

Cal, Daeg and Tag had started out with the one dive shop, Deep Dive, but had recently expanded. Cal had purchased half of the neighboring dive business, Dream Big and Dive, which meant he was now in partnership with Piper. Deep Dive was gradually focusing more on adventure diving, advanced training, and search and rescue, while Piper's dive shop handled more of the day-to-day dives. So they weren't competitors. They were playing for the same team, and her competitive urge could stand down.

The woman working on Dream Big's chalkboard turned around and waved hello. She was a pixie, brown hair piled up on top of her head in one of those gravity-defying twists Mia had never mastered. She also had a coffee can full of colored chalk that she was using to write out the day's specials.

"You must be Mia. I'm Carla—the assistant manager at Dream Big and Dive." Carla held out her hand, looked down at her pink-and-green fingers and hesitated. With a shrug, she wiped her hand on her jeans and tried again.

"Guilty as charged."

"Discovery Island's a small place." Carla flashed her a grin. "There's no keeping secrets here. For example, I hear our last resident bad-boy rescue swimmer is officially off the market. Congratulations."

Since the truth of their fake engagement was one secret she needed to keep, the island grapevine wasn't welcome news. Somehow, everything seemed more complicated now that it wasn't just the two of them facing down Ellie Damiano. The old woman had been funny. And sweet in a crazy way. But this was way more than she'd signed on for…

She stared at her whiteboard while Carla added an orange shark to her own chalkboard. Then she looked down at her black marker, which was not cutting it in the bling-and-flash department. She needed color. Out of space, Carla ambled over and stood next to her. Streaks of pink chalk decorated her cheek and her jeans. She examined Mia's sign and the neat block lettering.

"It's…very even." She sounded doubtful.

Yes, Mia's sign was certainly that. It was also legible and could be read from the end of the block. She looked back at Carla's handiwork. The other woman's work was…flamboyant. You'd probably have to be six inches away in order to figure out the prices and what was on offer, but it made her want to look. Slowing down and taking a second glance wasn't necessarily a bad thing.

"I'm ordering a chalkboard," she decided.

Carla grinned. "Easy peasy. You're sleeping with the owner. That ought to be good for unlimited office supplies." Wow. Mia blinked.

"Sorry." Carla made a face and purloined the black marker. "I'm missing my filter when it's this early. I probably shouldn't have assumed you're sleeping together. I mean, you could have a really traditional engagement."

"Maybe Tag's saving himself for our wedding night," she said dryly.

Carla snorted.

"That would be a total waste, wouldn't it?"

"Yeah," Cara agreed. "Speaking of which...Cal's promised to hire more rescue swimmers." She waggled her eyebrows. "You need to look out for your fellow females and make sure he hires more hotties. Since you took the last one, it's your civic responsibility to ensure he restocks."

"You make him sound like a cookie."

Granted, the man was edible. It was positively unfair how downright sexy he was. Having met Cal and Daeg, she could also see Carla's point. If the Navy had more sexy guys like these three, why not bring them to the island?

"I'm pretty sure federal labor laws say we can't hire people just because they're sexy."

The grin on Carla's face grew wider. "Modeling agencies do it all the time. We could have an all-military, all-hottie dive shop. Think of the business we'd get."

The door opened and Tag stepped outside. She hadn't realized he'd arrived. "Are we committing felonies before I've had coffee?"

He looked sinfully good. His wet suit was pushed

down to his waist and he wore another one of those ratty Navy T-shirts he loved so much. Mia was pretty sure he had a dozen of the same shirts and just rotated them. He wrapped an arm around her waist and drew her up against his side. He was warm and strong, and a whisper of awareness skittered through her. Clearly, there were already fringe benefits for her to enjoy from their "engagement."

That being said, her visceral reaction to seeing Tag in one piece and on the ground shook her. Part of her wanted to throw her arms around him and plant a kiss on his mouth. But touching wasn't part of their deal. He'd hired her to be his office manager, and keeping it professional was important. Bedroom things stayed in the bedroom. Or on the floor. Against the wall. Now that she thought about it, they hadn't spent anywhere near enough time in bed.

An oversight she'd have to remedy tonight when she got him alone.

"The rescue went well?" The relaxed but tired look on his face said it had, but Mia wanted to hear him say it.

"Got them all back safe and sound," he told her, dropping a kiss on her forehead.

"Hey." Carla gave him a friendly smack on the shoulder. "Congratulations."

"Thanks." Tag plucked the chalk out of the other woman's hand. "I'm pretty sure today's dive doesn't involve man-eating squid or..." He squinted. "A school of oarfish?"

"Barracuda. Tell my boss to send me to art school and you'll get better results." Carla grinned unrepentantly and pointed to Mia's hand. "When are you picking out the ring?"

"Spending my money, are ya?"

"Doing Mia here a favor. I want her on my side."

"You just want me to hire more Navy rescue swimmers," Mia said.

They hadn't talked about a ring. In fact, if she was being honest, they hadn't done much talking at all. When she and Tag were sharing air space, the chemistry between them took over. There tended to be a whole lot of kissing—which she was definitely a fan of—but not so much rational discussion. They probably should have figured out the parameters of their new "relationship" right away. However, buying a real ring for a fake relationship seemed like overkill in the window-dressing department.

Carla laughed. "*Hot* Navy rescue swimmers, remember? And there's already a poll going around as to who's going to have the biggest ring—you, Dani or Piper. Cal's pretty competitive, so keep that in mind."

"Will do," Tag said smoothly. "I'll plan on giving Mia here an absolute Mount Everest of a ring."

Cal stuck his head out of the dive shop. "Somebody made coffee. I drank it."

"Hey." Tag looked wounded. "She's my fiancée. That makes it *my* coffee."

"Ask me nicely and I'll make more." Since the men had spent the better part of the night and the wee hours searching for lost fishermen, coffee was the least she could do. She went back inside and fired up a second pot.

Cal slapped Tag on the back. "Coffee. She's a keeper. Good hire."

She shoved a cup of coffee in Tag's direction. Kissing could come later.

"Thanks." His fingers brushed hers as he took it. Those fingers had skimmed over her ribs, painting erotic circles on her skin. Her breasts. And lower...

"You're welcome." Please *and* thank you? Really? Manners were good, but this was an inane conversation to be having with all this heat and need pumping through her body. She'd planned and executed multi-team campaigns in the desert. She'd come under fire more than once and kept her cool. She'd led convoys and scanned the edges of highways for the signs of IEDs. She sighed. True, she wasn't entirely sure how she'd ended up on coffee detail, but sometimes the little things counted most, and hours of flying and swimming took it out of you. So if her contribution needed to be coffee, then that was the contribution she'd be making.

The way he raked his eyes over her confirmed her impression she looked good. Granted, FedEx's deliveries had plenty to do with her success in the good looks department, because her credit card had been working overtime. She'd paired a sassy little short-sleeved jacket with red fringe and enormous red flowers over a fitted white blouse and a denim skirt. Her espadrilles made her almost as tall as him. Fun stuff. No more khaki and creases for her. He flicked the fringe.

"Nice." He was tired and salty, his hair sticky from his swim as he grinned up at her. Something inside her turned over. *Just sex*, she reminded herself. *Nothing more.* Cal and Daeg filed in behind him, already discussing the day's agenda. *See? It's business as usual.*

Daeg eyeballed their calendar. "Damn. We need to hire more guys."

Mia toasted Daeg with her own coffee cup. "And gals."

Daeg looked over at her and flashed her a thumbs-up. "Point taken."

Okay. Her role here was marginally larger than coffee.

Tag looked at her. "Do you miss it?"

"It?"

"The missions. Going in hot and getting a job done. Doing stuff that matters."

"A job doesn't have to involve bullets and life-and-death to matter."

He exhaled "No, it doesn't, although I've personally found it helps."

"Good. Because there are plenty of people here on Discovery Island doing *stuff* that matters."

"I don't want to fight," he said gruffly, moving closer.

She knew it didn't look like anything out of the ordinary to the other guys in the office. In fact, she was pretty sure Daeg had his head down on his desk and was napping. Nearby Cal worked the phone, handling paperwork and logistics. She didn't care because, nope, she was too aware of the rescue swimmer horning in on her space.

"Okay."

He waited a beat. "Everything went well here?"

Yeah. She fought the urge to roll her eyes at him. *Office equipment was* so *life threatening.* She'd sorted and filed. She'd also made a dozen phone calls and probably spent the GDP of a small African country on Post-it notes and folders. Tag appeared to be a big fan of the heap system. He had heaps of papers on his desk. In the drawers. And, yes, in the shop's kitchen. At least she hadn't found anything in the bathroom. Yet. The day was still young, and she was working weekends because the man was so disorganized.

She pointed to the labeled, stickered stack near his elbow. "Those are the ones you need to deal with immediately. The rest can wait until tomorrow."

He grinned drolly at her. "I don't want to do paperwork, Mia. That's why we've got you."

Yeah. The mountainous proportions of his heaps had made his *need* perfectly clear. She wasn't stupid—just organized.

"You'll thank me when the electric company doesn't turn off your power."

"The power bill is Cal's responsibility."

"Nice try. He said pretty much the same thing to me. You lose."

He ran a hand over his head. He did look tired, and she knew she wasn't helping. But he'd hired her to do a job, and she'd do it.

Or not.

"Give me the checkbook." She held out a hand. "I'll do it."

He hesitated, shooting a glance toward Cal. Daeg let out a rasping sigh, still down for the count. No back up there.

Pinning Cal with a no-nonsense stare, she asked, "Do you have a problem with my paying bills?"

Cal shrugged. "If Tag's cool with it, so am I."

"Cop out." Tag groaned.

"You hired her."

True. She wondered how Tag had explained their knowing each other. It didn't matter. She was staying on task here. She waggled her fingers.

"Give it up."

Tag yanked open his desk drawer. Since she'd had spare time, she'd organized the contents. Now his pencils were lined up on the left, with pens only on the right. "Jesus."

"I'm going to assume that's a prayer of thanksgiving." She had no idea how he'd ever managed to find anything in there.

He leaned in, big and rough and sexy. "Let's recap. Who's the boss here?"

He was either playing with her, or he was genuinely bent out of shape because she'd touched his office supplies. Her money was on option A. But since he was tired, she'd cut him some slack.

"You're signing my paychecks," she said cheerfully.

"That's what I thought."

"You told me to stay busy," she reminded him. "And your record-keeping is a disgrace."

Shaking his head, he pulled the drawer out farther and pointed. To underscore the fact she was a team player, she made a point of looking. Everything was exactly as she'd left it. Neat and ordered. Square and lined up. *Perfect*. He could definitely thank her now.

"Your Post-its look like they're on drill."

"You can also find them," she pointed out.

"I don't recall giving you permission to touch my things."

Right. "I didn't know I needed *permission*."

"Mia—" God, she loved the way he said her name. "I am your boss."

"In the office." She could play games, too. Slowly she walked her fingers up his muscular chest and hooked a finger in the collar of his T-shirt. "So you'd better make the most of it, big guy."

JESUS. SHE LOOKED at him and he—he wanted to give her whatever she wanted. Unzip her sassy little skirt and explore all her secret spots. He eyeballed the room, assessing the feasibility of his ad-hoc plan. Daeg had his head down on his desk, and, from the rough sounds emanating from his friend's vicinity, the guy was out for a while. Cal wouldn't be rescuing him, either. Still busy arguing with someone, he was headed out the front, ear glued to his cell. Yeah. If he was looking for backup, he wasn't finding it there. He was free to fall unchecked for Mia.

Pity, he couldn't afford it.

She'd declared herself to be a stay-put kind of gal—and he was headed back for San Diego and a new mission in a few weeks. The problem was, he had absolutely no willpower around Mia. She tugged at his shirt, a quick, determined no-nonsense kind of pull. He let her reel him in. He didn't want to keep his hands off her, and she seemed to share his opinion.

Which was why his mouth had ended up hovering mere inches above hers in dangerous territory. "You like to be in charge."

She smiled and crossed her legs, her bare knee brushing his. Her denim skirt inched upward. If he ran a hand up her leg, the denim would ruck right up, leaving her bare.

"You're playing with fire," he growled.

Instead of retreating, *of course* she tilted her head up until her lower lip brushed against his. Jesus. Was that her tongue?

"I've got it on good authority you know how to rescue a woman."

"Whatever you want," he croaked. If Daeg weren't

here, he'd have her on the desk, and that was wrong. He didn't want his body making promises his heart couldn't keep. Staying on Discovery Island was out of the question. He'd signed contracts, made a commitment to his CO. He'd never questioned his decision before, but now…he wondered. Hell, yeah, he wondered.

"This." The word became a whisper as her mouth closed in on his. So, damn it, for a long, sweet moment he let her kiss him.

She nipped him then, her hands cupping the back of his head as she lifted her mouth off his. "Don't make me do all the work here, sailor."

More orders. He scooped her up, pulling her onto his lap until she straddled him. Damned if her skirt wasn't made for the position.

"Just kisses?" His breathing sounded rough as he asked. Only to clarify, because it was important to know where he stood. Sat. Whatever. *Danger.*

She snuck a peek at Daeg. He could have told her the man slept like the dead. Plus, they'd been up all night. It was a minor miracle any of them were still standing.

"Just kisses."

He flattened his palm against her heart, savoring the urgent drumbeat. She wanted him, and her need was sexy as hell.

"You're kissing your boss."

He leaned in and flicked a button open.

"You can't undress me here." She was positively cute when she was shocked.

"Who's the boss?" He kissed her again to distract her while he flicked buttons two and three open. Her bra was downright wicked—lavender-and-white checks with a strip of sweet, innocent lace outlining her curves. "I like this."

"I'll bet you do," she muttered, shooting an anxious look over at Daeg.

"You could take it off," he suggested.

"You have a boss-secretary fetish."

No, he had a *thing* for Mia. He undid one more button. White cotton gaped away from her silky skin and that damned bra. If she was a secretary, she was a very, very naughty secretary indeed. He wrapped his hand around her thigh.

"Are we agreed?"

"What?" She sounded breathless. *Good.*

He eased his palm up her thigh.

"That I'm in charge."

When he slid a finger beneath her thong, she was wet and slick. And he wasn't, he realized, feeling nice. One quick, hard tug and her panties were his.

"Tag." She froze, as if she couldn't believe he'd done what he'd done and in the middle of the office. Well, that made two of them, but she drove him crazy.

"This is why I'm in charge." He stroked deeper.

She made an unintelligible noise, part moan, part breathy sigh.

"You're mine," he said and stroked her again. He could do this for hours, easing her higher. Unfortunately, Daeg stirred, his boots banging against his desk, and the dazed look in her eyes faded.

She slid off his lap and glared at him, holding out her hand for her panties.

"This can't be anything more than a game. I'm not interested in any kind of a long-distance *thing*. I had one of those and it didn't end well."

"I didn't know I was a *thing*," he muttered after a long moment. His words didn't come out right, but he also had no intention of returning her panties. Instead, he tucked them into his back pocket.

"A really, really good thing. A sexual thing. Like brownies with chocolate sauce and whipped cream and that little red cherry thing, but right after your doctor tells you to lose twenty pounds."

He looked her up and down as she buttoned up her shirt. "You look fine to me."

Understatement.

"I can't let you be my *thing*," she reiterated fiercely. "Because you're leaving and going back to San Diego and the Navy."

"And what are *you* doing?"

"I'm still figuring it out." His skeptical glance must have said it all because she continued. "I have a plan."

Of course she did. "That's what I mean. And I'll bet your plan is in writing, color coded with action items and deliverable dates. It's not a plan—it's a step-by-step diagram of how to take over the world."

"You think I'm bossy."

It might be true, but he didn't need to *agree*. Ignoring her indignant look, he shrugged. "Too bad," he said.

"Excuse me?"

"Because I'd make sure I was worth waiting for. You ever had welcome-home sex?" He had no idea why he was arguing with her. He didn't want a *thing* with her, either. Absolutely not.

He did up her bottommost button, then ran his finger up to the next one.

"Or been so hot you can't wait until you're home so you do it in the car?"

"Pass," she said, but she didn't sound certain at all. He did up another button. She sounded *aroused*.

"Liar," he whispered against her mouth, tracing his finger over her skin to the next button. "You don't fantasize about your soldier coming home, dropping his gun on the bedside table, and ravishing you?"

"Because you'd be happy to bring my fantasies to life?"

Her question wasn't a *no*.

"Uh-huh. We could do a boss fantasy," he murmured, slipping his finger between her breasts. "I'll buy a conference room table. We could combine it with soldier-comes-home."

"How are you with the knight-in-shining-armor fantasy? You can worship me from afar and keep your hands to yourself." She did up the last button on her blouse.

"Uh-uh," he told her. "And, since I'm the boss, I get what I want."

"Definitely a fantasy," she said sweetly and held out her hand. "I want my panties back."

Too bad for his sergeant she wasn't getting what she wanted. Of course, since *he* wasn't getting what *he* wanted, it seemed only fair.

11

CLOSING ON THE cottage turned out to be easy. Two weeks after she'd first laid eyes on the place, she was the proud possessor of a deed and two keys to the front door. The bank had also approved her home equity line, and she'd probably purchased enough supplies to open her own Home Depot store. Moving out of Tag's place might have caused her a little pang somewhere in the region of her heart, but theirs had been a temporary arrangement.

Bought a house, she texted Laurel, knowing her cousin would be excited for her. Despite her love of bling, Laurel had chosen to sport a small-size rock on her ring finger because she and Jack were saving up for a down payment on a home. Trading carats for an extra bedroom had been an easy call.

Photos now! Laurel responded, and Mia spent the next half hour happily trading decorating ideas. When someone knocked on her door, she wasn't prepared to see Tag standing there holding a box of painting supplies. She supposed he wanted to help. Bonus points for him.

"Are you the Welcome Wagon?" Because she could think of all sorts of ways—deliciously sexy, very naughty ways—to break in her new house. She hadn't had her hands on Tag for almost twenty-four hours, and she was definitely going through serious withdrawal.

He waved the box at her. "I swung by the hardware store before I came here. Thought maybe you could use a hand…"

"Are you implying I don't know how to paint my own walls?" Because, really, she was a modern woman. She knew her way around a toolbox—and YouTube.

He propped the box against his hip and grinned at her. "Have you painted interiors before?"

She had the internet. She'd repainted her bedroom in high school. Both of which made her fully qualified. She opened her mouth to say so, but then she got a good look at Tag. He was wearing a faded T-shirt and a ragged pair of blue jeans. God, she loved worn jeans on a guy. There was always the possibility his pants would just give out while he was lovingly bent over a paint can. A gal could hope.

She opened the door. "Come on in. It must be my lucky day."

Yep. Suspicion filled his eyes. Maybe he'd sensed her rip-his-clothes-off fantasy. "What have you done with Mia?"

"Excuse me?"

He brushed past her when she didn't move out of the door. "I didn't expect you to *agree*. Not that quickly."

Since he seemed determined to invade her house, she followed him, tugging at the back of his shirt. Which stayed firmly on his magnificent body, more was the pity. "I like free labor."

He gave her The Look. "Now you're taking advantage of me."

She shrugged. Yeah…she probably was taking advantage here. However, she had a house to paint, and he was hot. That was called *having her cake and eating it, too.* "I'm perfectly happy to let you help me paint. The question is—what's in it for you?"

"I'm just being a doting fiancé." He flashed her a grin and nodded toward the living room. "Are we starting in there?"

The thing was, he wasn't really her fiancé, and they both knew it. They had some kind of complicated pretend relationship going on, more like friends with benefits. She wasn't really dating him or settling down with him or doing anything other than sleeping with him. And there wasn't even much *sleeping* involved because she couldn't seem to keep her hands off him. Nope, she was just passing herself off as his betrothed to get the good folks of Discovery Island off his back. Any pleasure she got out of the fantasy was pure bonus.

The former owner must have harbored a secret desire to open an art gallery, because the living room walls were dotted with holes from long-AWOL picture frames. After the tenth spackle-and-patch job, Tag looked over at her.

"Are you sure you can't just hang new pictures up over the holes?"

"Don't be such a slacker." She wanted to do it right.

"You've got issues." He sounded cheerful. "I should charge you by the hour."

"You work for sex. You come cheap," Mia reminded him. She could have hired a painting crew, but she wanted to do as much of the work as she could, and not just because she wanted to preserve her line of credit. This was *her* house, her fresh start, and she'd make it perfect. Or—she eyed her lumpy spackle job—near-perfect. She'd hang a picture on this spot.

"You can make it up to me later," he said.

She'd just bet she could. In fact, her imagination suggested a dozen perfectly naughty, wonderfully decadent things she could do to him.

"Besides, this may be my last chance to paint walls for a while."

Right. Because he was leaving. She was pretty sure painting wasn't part of his job description for Uncle Sam, unless it involved painting a target.

"You don't want to stick around now that the business is finally getting off the ground?" she asked casually.

"Hell, no. I'm not the kind of person who settles down. My idea of a good time is jumping out of a helicopter feet-first into shark-infested waters. It makes me a good story at a bar, but bad long-term material."

He didn't sound like he cared, which was an important reminder for her.

"Funny," she said. "You should have thought of that before you proposed."

He gave her the *be serious* look. "Why did you join the Army?"

"Because Uncle Sam wanted me?"

"Mia." And there it was—his growly voice, the one that made her think about dragging him off to bed, even when it really, really wasn't a good idea. They wanted different things from their lives, which was perfectly fine, except she was also starting to think she might want *him* in her life. As more than her fake fiancé.

"My whole family joined. It's what we do. My father served. My three brothers served. I served. They took some convincing when I told them it was my turn."

He nodded and slapped more paint on her walls. She'd picked the color because it reminded her of an enormous bowl of oranges, bold and citrusy. He wasn't done with his questions, though.

"Why didn't you leave Discovery Island like you'd planned?"

She edged her paintbrush neatly along the white trim, loving the way the ribbon of bright orange brought out the creamy paleness of the wood. "I meant to leave, but I fell in love. Is that so surprising? Cal and Daeg liked it enough to stay. Maybe you'll change your mind, too."

God, she shouldn't have said those last few words. Because they both knew she wasn't playing, not entirely. Between the house and the man, she was definitely falling in love. She'd needed his help—whether she'd wanted to admit it out loud or not—and he'd swooped in to rescue her. But that was the thing about rescues— they were one-time emergencies. Rescues didn't happen on a daily basis, and, frankly, she wouldn't want them to. She wanted a relationship.

With Tag.

Who was leaving in a matter of weeks.

"I'm not them," he said impatiently. "Daeg and Cal have Deep Dive and their fiancées. Cal has family here and Daeg practically grew up with them. That's not me. That's not who I am. My CO needs me."

She needed him.

Mia waved a hand impatiently. Droplets of orange paint hit the front of his T-shirt and speckled his cheek. *Oops.* "What do you need, Tag?"

"A clean shirt," he groused, his voice low and husky. He took a step toward her, and she was pretty certain the rest of her living room wasn't getting painted today, because he reached out and stroked his own brush down the valley between her breasts.

"You could take it off," she said breathlessly.

"Mmm. Or you could tell me what *you* need." His brush painted a wicked circle over her left nipple. She wondered what he would do if she told him the truth, that she needed him to stay put and be a long-term part of her life. He'd probably be on the next ferry out of Discovery Island. With apologies, of course, because Tag was a genuinely nice guy.

"You," she said, winding her arms around his neck and trapping his brush between them. Painting could definitely wait. "I need you. Stay."

He stared at her and she had no idea what he saw. But he'd been the one touching her breast, so surely that meant he was interested. That she hadn't misunderstood.

"Mia?"

"Yeah?" God. He moved his hand, the brush. *Something.* Nerve ends sprang to life in her breasts. They should definitely do more of this.

"I can stay tonight," he said, gently reminding her of their limits. He'd be hers for tonight and possibly the next few weeks as well but, eventually, he'd go. She could work with that.

"Stay," she said again, dragging his head down to hers.

"Can we borrow your bed?" He didn't wait for an answer, swinging her up into his arms and heading for her bedroom.

"Too old for the floor?" She pushed the door open for him, and he took her straight inside, setting her down on her feet by the edge of the mattress.

"You have no idea," he rasped, "what you do to me, do you?"

Nope, but she loved the husky groan he gave when he slid her shirt off. Since she hadn't bothered with a bra, his move left her breasts bare. Her *orange* breasts. The paint from Tag's brush had sunk through her tank top. She thought about possibilities for a moment and then decided she didn't care if they got paint on the bed. She could always buy new sheets. She wanted him out of control and she wanted that now.

He ran his fingers over the paint-streaked tops of her breasts.

"You're gorgeous."

"Not as gorgeous as you," she said throatily.

"Men aren't gorgeous." He peeled her shorts and her panties down as he said it, stripping her bare for him. "I'd far rather look at you."

"Hmm. You definitely are here." She leaned in, pressing her mouth against the spot on his throat where his pulse beat out a sexy rhythm. Then she moved lower, pushing his shorts and his boxers down his legs.

"*Hello.* And most definitely here." She wrapped her palm around him, and the taut muscles in his stomach jumped in happy anticipation. Since she still didn't have him quite where she wanted him, she pushed him down onto the edge of the bed. "Can I have my wicked way with you?"

"Don't let me stop you. Please." She could hear the smile in his voice, so she dropped to her knees between his legs and took him in her mouth.

He groaned, the harsh, needy noise thrilling her. When she looked up at him through her lashes, he was watching her take him, and the raw desire on his face was almost as big of a turn-on as the feel of him. He threaded his fingers through her hair, holding on and making her feel powerful and sexy. *Needed…*

Good behavior definitely deserved a reward. She sucked her way up his thick shaft, swirling the point of her tongue over the spot just beneath the head.

"I'm happy to paint with you anytime," he rasped.

"Good to know. I have a big house." She smiled against him, then licked him.

Once. Twice. She cupped him, rubbing him with the palm of her hand where she couldn't cover him with her mouth. The move earned her a sexy growl from her man, so she did it again, exploring every inch of him with her tongue.

He fell backward onto the bed, tugging her with him.

"Hey." She nipped his ear. "I was busy."

"I know," he groaned. "But I'm not going to last much longer."

Fine with her. Together they rolled on a condom, and then he was flipping her underneath him, pinning her to the mattress. Kissing her mouth, her throat, her ear as he fitted himself against her opening and pushed slowly in.

"Tag?"

"Right here," he muttered, sinking in deeper.

Oh, yeah.

"I—" She forgot what she was trying to say because he kissed her some more, and then he moved. She panted and twisted, and someone who sounded a whole lot like her was chanting *more more more* in a hoarse, whimpering voice that might have embarrassed her if he hadn't made her feel so good. But this was Tag. Her friend. Letting him know what she needed was okay.

He lifted her up, cupping her bottom, and she grabbed his butt. Their hips slammed together, and then it got loud and messy and perfect. He stroked deep inside her body, until they were skin on skin, hip to hip, her breasts squashed against his chest, his dog tags tickling her throat. The delicious friction built, pulling her slowly apart with the pleasure of it until she came, and he followed her over the edge.

Afterward, she lay there in a boneless heap by his side. He curved an arm around her and fished for the sheet with his foot. She was pretty sure the roof of her new cottage could have caved in, and she wouldn't have cared.

"Wow."

"Right there with you." He cleared his throat but then said nothing more. How did anyone find words to describe what they'd just done? Instead, he just held her close, and his touch was even better than talking.

When she was just drifting off to sleep, he ran a finger down her spine. "Mia?"

"Yeah?"

"What kind of a ring do you want?"

She tried to see his face, but now the room was getting dark. Picking out a ring for a fake engagement seemed over-the-top. "We don't need a ring. Maybe I'm really, really modern and don't believe in jewelry."

"Or you're the kind of woman who gets her man a ring, since if she's wearing one, he does, too." He stroked his hand up her back, his fingertips grazing her shoulders.

She kind of liked the sound of that.

"The whole island is taking bets on what kind of ring you're going to be wearing. It's easier to just get something now and let them find something else to talk about."

She could feel his penetrating gaze on her. She didn't know what he was looking for, what she was supposed to say. She didn't mind wearing his ring, although it felt like a cheat. *Play it off.* They were friends with benefits. Nothing more.

"I should make you guess. Isn't that a fiancée kind of thing to do?"

"If you want something ugly, sure. What do *you* like?" He rolled over and propped his head on his hands.

You.

I like you.

She'd never been one for jewelry. The military had strict rules on what was appropriate and what was not. She'd been limited to a simple pair of matched studs for her ears and a wristwatch. If she'd been married, she could have worn her wedding band and engagement ring, although sporting bling in the sandbox would have been dangerous.

"I don't know." How sad was that? "But nothing real."

"Mia." He exhaled roughly. "You have to be the first woman in history who prefers cubic zirconia."

"There's nothing wrong with being practical."

"Should I surprise you?"

"Go for it," she said.

But the funny thing was: he already had.

12

PAINTING HAD BEEN undeniably fun, even if she still had two bare walls. The memories kept Mia smiling right through the next day. She seemed to smile a lot around Tag. He'd gone back to his place that morning because he had his menagerie to feed. Meanwhile, Mia had a fixer-upper to wrestle into shape, not to mention a garage full of boxes from her mainland storage unit to tackle, so she should have been busting her ass.

But instead, she was sitting on her front porch, actually contemplating getting into the blue plastic kid's pool she'd discovered in her new shed. Discovery Island had been hit with a late heat wave, and odds were high she'd melt before sunset. Laurel had also packed up and forwarded Mia's stranded things from the cruise ship, military-care-package style…and had added a few bonus toys. *Sex toys for the rescue-swimmer hottie*, or so the handwritten note had said. Laurel had also included some lingerie the likes of which Mia had never seen before. Apparently, her cousin had been showered with a wedding-night bonanza—or had gone on a shopping spree—that ought to make Tag a happy man.

Painting and patching paled in comparison to the fantasies she was cooking up.

Movement caught her eye, causing a momentary spike of adrenaline. Mia's breath returned to normal when she realized it was Piper, Cal's fiancée and the co-owner of Dream Big and Dive, striding up the path.

"How's engaged life?" she asked, barely masking her mischievous smile. Mia had only met the young woman a couple of times, but she already liked her. Dani, Daeg's fiancée, and Carla trailed behind Piper, waving paper grocery bags that looked suspiciously like they contained at least ten thousand calories of carbs and sugar.

Thank God.

"I haven't killed him yet," she deadpanned. That was a definite win in her book and underscored the wisdom of having a practice fiancé. When she got around to the real deal, she'd be prepared.

Not.

"Bonus points for you," Piper said solemnly. "Cal and I make a point of fighting at least once a week. Plus, makeup sex is the best."

Behind her, Carla made a face. Piper's dive shop assistant manager was a hoot, and Mia looked forward to getting to know her better. When Tag had told her Piper and Dani knew the truth about their engagement, she'd worried they would be unhappy about the deception, but her worry had turned out to be unfounded.

Completely unfounded.

They simply wanted to convert her sham engagement into the real deal.

Carla waved a hand in protest. "TMI. All sex must be discussed in the abstract."

Piper grinned, unrepentant. "You're just jealous."

"Absolutely." Carla dropped her bag on the porch. "And I also have zero desire to look at Cal and think 'He and Piper did it doggy style in the kitchen!' For one thing, I'd never be able to eat at your place again."

Mia looked over at Dani. "Is this a hypothetical situation, or did it actually happen?"

Dani threw up her hands. "I'm not asking because Piper here wouldn't have any problem with *telling*. Don't share anything with her that you don't want broadcast all over the island."

Piper stuck out her tongue, laughing. "I'll bet you've got all sorts of amazing stories from working at Sweet Moon's. Your grandparents' motel is where everyone on the island goes when they want a little romantic time alone."

Right. Time for a distraction. Mia pointed to two shopping bags with her borrowed wardrobe on the front porch. "I've got your things clean and ready for you. Thanks for lending them to me."

She'd had the rest of her stuff shipped in a PODS unit that had arrived yesterday from the mainland.

Piper peered inside. "Wow. You could totally start a laundry service. I'd be the first to sign up."

So she liked things neat and tidy—those were admirable qualities. "I appreciate the loan."

"No problem." Piper grinned, eyeing the pool and the hose. "I think I came out ahead on this one. Are we having a pool party?"

Why not? An hour later, Piper had filled the plastic pool with the hose, and Mia had dragged out a cooler full of frozen drink pouches. She had both piña colada and peach daiquiri. Go her. She also made a mean tuna-fish sandwich and now they were lounging on her porch in bikinis, with their feet in the pool. It wasn't a power lunch in suits, but there was plenty of laughter.

Carla stabbed her drink pouch with a straw, slurping happily. "So how did you really meet Tag? When you weren't rescuing him from matchmaking old ladies, that is."

She looked at Piper and Dani. "Carla knows, too?" Was there anyone who *didn't* know?

"It's hard to keep secrets," Piper said apologetically.

"And I'm completely trustworthy," Carla added.

Confession time. "We met in San Diego, when we both had leave. At a bar."

There was no point in leaving out the gory details, right?

"He was a bar hookup? You rock." Piper high-fived her.

"You should keep him," Dani suggested.

Mia inhaled her drink and choked.

Piper whacked her on the back. "Not a good idea?"

"It's a *fake* engagement. Hello. That means we're not getting married. We're not a couple."

"Yeah, but you're having real sex, right?"

Yep. She was blushing. She could ride in a Jeep with soldiers sharing the raunchiest sex jokes, but apparently she turned beet-red if the sex life in question was her own. Way to go, soldier. "Tag doesn't want a fiancée."

"He doesn't *know* he wants one," Dani countered. "He's a guy, so he needs a nudge."

"Are you matchmaking?" Because that was what had gotten her into this mess in the first place.

"Maybe." Piper grinned unrepentantly. "We like you. We like Tag. See? Match made in heaven."

"I was engaged before. It didn't work out so well." Possibly, she should check the alcohol content on her drink, because she had no idea where those words had come from.

"Do tell." After producing a polka-dot bikini from somewhere, Piper had proceeded to commandeer the pool. She lay in the center, her legs sprawled over its plastic edge. With her big white sunglasses, she looked very Marilyn Monroe.

"Yeah." Carla nudged Mia hopefully. "Take pity on us single girls and share. At the very least, give me the name of the bar so Deep Dive can import more single men from there. The dating pool on this island is pathetic."

Before she could answer, however, a truck pulled up in front of the cottage, and Daeg and Cal got out. Piper abandoned her spot in the pool, plastering herself against Cal. Partly, Mia suspected, to get her fiancé soaking wet and partly to kiss him hello. Dani followed suit, winding herself around Daeg. Mia doubted her front yard had ever seen so many torrid kisses. Holy. Moly.

"We're odd women out." Carla sighed. "It's disgusting, isn't it? Let me buy you another daiquiri."

Mia took the frozen pouch Carla pulled out of the cooler. Unlike Carla, she wanted *that*—the something she saw in Cal and Daeg's faces when they looked at their fiancées—and *that* wasn't something she could simply order into being.

"We're thinking a Vegas wedding," Piper said happily, when Cal let her come up for air.

"I didn't get the memo this was a party."

Her traitorous heart thumped, lurching into overtime. Tag strode up her garden path, looking rumpled and sexy. He'd brought more fix-it supplies, along with Ben Franklin, the boxer, who happily helped himself to a drink from the pool and then picked out a shady spot underneath a hydrangea. Cal pulled her into a one-sided hug, catching her hand in his. "You leave this finger bare too long, and someone might make a move on her."

Daeg tugged her in his direction. "X marks the spot?"

"Sure and why don't you all just pee on her yard?" Carla quipped, eliciting a chorus of groans.

Mia hopped into the pool, taking Piper's abandoned spot. Screw it. She didn't care if Ben Franklin had just used it as a water fountain. She was pretty certain there wasn't a sink in her house Sam hadn't drunk out of. Maybe the cold water would cool down her feelings for Tag.

Or not.

Keep him.

Like he'd read her mind, he set down his box of stuff and headed her way, pulling his T-shirt over his head. A pair of swim trunks hung temptingly low on his hips. She looked up—reluctantly—and over the hard lines of his abdomen. He grinned down at her, a sensual smile tugging at his lips. "Budge up."

Her wading pool was hardly built for two. "No room at the inn. The ocean is to your right about a hundred yards. Try there."

"Uh-huh." He scooped her up into his arms before she could protest and dropped down into the pool, cradling her against his chest. "Jesus. That's cold."

"Baby."

In retaliation, he dropped her into the water, but, since she ended up cradled between his legs, his arms wrapped around her middle while their friends catcalled and hollered encouragement, his penance was no penance at all. In fact, she rather suspected her heart was melting faster than her daiquiri in the sun.

13

THE FERRY BACK to Discovery Island left in an hour. Tag had already bought the ticket and parked his truck in the growing queue. All he had to do now was pick up a ring before it was time to board. Conveniently, the drugstore nearest the pier had trays of inexpensive rings in the front window. The rings were cheerful and packed plenty of glitter.

He fought the urge to look over his shoulder like 007. The odds of anyone watching him duck into the drugstore for a fake ring were low. He could be in and out in under ten minutes, and it wasn't like they had a real engagement. After all, she'd told him to buy cubic zirconia.

Doing anything else was stupid.

But they had something. He wasn't sure what that something was, and he only had a few weeks left to explore it. He was an idiot, but he looked down the street anyhow, and, sure enough, the jewelry store was right where he'd noticed it when he'd driven his truck off the ferry earlier today.

There was really only one reason to buy a ring for a

woman: because he wanted to. Despite their Discovery Island peanut gallery, the ring was for her. For them. But she'd wanted to keep it casual. They were friends with benefits, she'd said.

He just hadn't expected his friendship with Mia to come with quite so many benefits. She was really hot in bed, although he'd known that for years. She was also funny and smart. She gave as good as she got, and he liked spending time with her. The fact he didn't mind picking out a ring for her said it all. She was more than just a friend or a benefit.

Damn it.

He should go inside the drugstore, grab the biggest, cheapest cubic zirconia ring he could find, and hightail it back to Discovery Island. They'd have a good laugh showing it off to curious onlookers and play it up to the hilt fielding questions about price tags and size compensation issues. His reflection grinned at him looking like a crazy man.

Except…

He wanted to do something nice for her, even if she didn't know about it. His feet were on board with the plan, turning and taking him down the sidewalk to the jeweler's. He pushed open the door and stepped inside. *Jesus.* Not his kind of place. The shop was dull of frou-frou glass cases and little velvet footstool things. Or maybe they were chairs. Hell if he knew.

The saleslady was already moving forward. "Can I help you?"

Yeah. I need a new brain.

"I need a ring," he said. "An engagement ring."

She beamed at him. "Are you surprising someone?"

She had no idea.

"You bet," he said gruffly.

The saleslady nodded as if he was Solomon the Wise and pointed him to one of those footstool things. "Sit."

Okay. So it was a chair. He sat.

After ten minutes of looking at rings and pretending he had a clue, he was in trouble. Who knew engagement rings came in anything but small, medium or large? He could disassemble an M16 in seconds and fly a Blackhawk through a shit storm. The difference between marquise-cut and princess-cut, however, was beyond him.

He grabbed his phone and thumbed through his contacts. He needed a female. One with engagement ring experience and an inside line on Mia's tastes. Maybe Piper could be his lifeline.

What does Mia like?

Then, in case Piper thought he was simply picking up sandwiches and not positively dying here, he added, in rings.

He poked a few rings while he waited for her response.

When it came, it was suitably enthusiastic.

Are you doing it? For real??!!!

I want to get her something nice, he texted back, trying to be subtle.

The saleslady pulled another tray. The rings looked ridiculous in the palm of his hand, all delicate and ethereal. He had no idea how Daeg had managed this. Too bad he didn't have a family heirloom he could pop out, but he was damned certain his mom was still attached to her rings, even though his dad hadn't been the biggest prize.

"It's hard to choose, isn't it?" The clerk gave him a sympathetic smile. "Just look for the one that winks at you."

He had no idea what she was talking about.

Classy, Piper texted. Simple. Elegant. Pick one.

A ring caught his eye, and he tugged it carefully out of its velvet nest. Some kind of pinky-gold, it had two rows of smaller diamonds like beads on a bracelet surrounding a big, round stone. He could imagine this ring on Mia's finger. It was warm and beautiful, and it...winked?

"This one. I'll take this one."

MIA HAD EXCELLENT REFLEXES. She caught the box Tag tossed her one-handed, without looking up from some spreadsheet she was working on. She'd brought order to the office, and he had a feeling she'd moved on to ordering him. Strangely, he didn't mind.

"You throw things at me, sailor, and I have good grounds for a hostile workplace lawsuit."

"It's a gift, not a hand grenade."

That made her look. "I know it's not my birthday. I don't think I've overlooked any major gift-giving holidays. Is it national secretary appreciation day?"

"Open it," he said gruffly.

She stuck her tongue out at him, which just made him think about other things she could do with it. Things like kissing. It was all too easy to imagine her pretty pink tongue tormenting him. Like she'd done last night, after her impromptu pool party had broken up and he'd taken her back inside. The soldiers he'd fought with could drink a bar dry. Not Mia. Two of those frozen girly drinks, and she'd been buzzed. She was cute when she wasn't quite sober.

He knew the minute she opened the box, because she froze and made a little noise he'd definitely never heard before. He didn't know why he cared if she liked his ring or not. It wasn't like they were really engaged, so he didn't need to figure out her ring size or whether she was more traditional or modern. Hell. He hadn't even known there were more than three kinds of engagement rings before his off-island visit had taught him rings came in all sorts of shapes and sizes.

The ring in the box was definitely a *large* and had cost him enough money to purchase a small car. A really, really good small car. But he'd looked at it in the jeweler's case and imagined it on her finger. She deserved a real ring, even if she didn't know it.

"It's…nice." She looked from the ring to him. "You're not going down on one knee? Isn't that how this is supposed to work?"

"You didn't tell me getting down on bended knee was part of the deal," he said. They had a fake engagement. If he'd gone and chosen a real ring, that was on him. When his phone buzzed, alerting him to a new email, he was glad for the excuse to look away as she took care of business, sliding the ring onto the appropriate finger.

His CO had sent him a status update. The team was meeting in San Diego in a week and a half. A week after that, they'd be deploying to South America.

"Thanks." Mia gazed down at the ring adorning her finger and then closed the box, tucking it inside that massive thing she called a bag. He could have packed the contents of his deployment duffel in there. He had no idea what it was with women and their purses, but Dani always had a similar oversize suitcase hanging off her shoulder.

"No problem." There was a moment of awkward silence, as if they both knew engagement rings required some kind of conversation. Probably he should have hit Cal and Daeg up for tips, although the pair would have teased him for the next twenty years or so.

"So," she said, pointing to his phone. The diamonds in her ring flashed, and he almost thought she was sneaking peeks at the band. But that wasn't Mia. Other than the handbag and the terrible taste in cocktails, she didn't have a girly bone in her body. That was why this thing between them worked so well. "Work crisis?"

"My CO." He didn't want to go into the details, but, fortunately, Mia already knew the drill. After all, she'd been the one shipping out for years.

"Pickup details?"

"Yeah." He could practically hear an invisible clock ticking down his remaining hours. Whatever this thing was with Mia, it was almost over. His replacement for Deep Dive would be arriving any day now, and he'd all but wrapped it up here. Restless, he got up and wandered out to the alley, where Daeg was rinsing off dive equipment. He had no idea what Cal was doing, but it seemed to involve leaning against the wall, watching Daeg work.

Cal looked up when he came out. "We got your replacement lined up. Sam Black will be here by Monday."

He'd bring the guy up to speed, then he'd turn in his keys to his landlord and board the ferry. Packing would be a ten-minute job, since he'd pretty much been living out of a single duffel bag.

Daeg dropped a load of fins into the tank. "Did Dr. Dolittle find homes for all of his animal companions?"

Cal's mother was taking the rabbit, and one of his sisters had fallen for Beauregard. Love at first sight, or so she'd claimed. The cat would be in good hands. The dogs…well, it turned out that Dani had a soft spot for them.

He flipped Daeg a two-fingered salute. "Congratulations. You're now the proud papa of a boxer and a Chihuahua."

In answer, Daeg turned the hose on him. "You need to stop rescuing so many damned animals or you're never leaving the island."

"People," Cal said. "That's his real problem. He rescues them, and then, two legs or four legs, he gets attached."

"Duly noted." Although rescuing Mia hadn't exactly been a hardship.

"So, you're good to go," Cal said.

Right. Good to go. His CO had tapped him for mission-critical work. Had offered him a chance to make a damned difference in the world. Mia knew where they stood, and he'd shipped out dozens of times before. This time shouldn't have felt any different. Shouldn't have *been* different.

"Yeah. I'm ready to hit the road," he agreed. Funny, though, how his head knew leaving was the right thing to do, but his heart hadn't quite gotten the message.

14

SOMEONE HAD ORDERED Tag a stack of extremely sexy "Billionaire Boss" books. Although Cal and Daeg had enjoyed the joke—and he now knew better than to open any package he hadn't ordered himself—Tag was pretty sure he was sleeping with the culprit. He'd taken them back to his place, flipped through the first pages of one, and somehow the next thing he'd known, it had been dark o'clock outside and Beauregard was acting like he hadn't been fed in at least one century. Or possibly two.

To show his appreciation, he'd marked the best spots with Post-it notes and considered depositing the stack on Mia's desk. Turnabout was only fair, after all. But... holy. Hell. Reading those steamy page-turners had definitely broadened his horizons, which was undoubtedly the reason he was standing on her front porch with the books tucked under his arm.

"You sent me a present," he said, when she opened the door. From somewhere inside the cottage, he heard the sound of running water. Apparently, he'd interrupted her en route to the shower.

"I might have and I'm glad to see you, too." She

smiled up at him, and he looked down at her mouth.
The sweet curve of her throat. Her breasts where they
peeked out above her black tank top. He'd seen her
naked more than once, but he couldn't imagine the day
he'd get tired of unwrapping her.

"Uh-huh." He dropped a quick, hard kiss on her
mouth. "If you confess, I'll go easier on you."

When he released the stack of books into her arms,
she grinned and stepped away from the door so he could
come in.

"I thought that since we'd established you're only
the boss of me in the office, I'd give you some food for
thought. You should see my *Cosmopolitan* collection."

He couldn't wait. He loved it when she was wicked.

"If you stayed here, you could read my magazines."
She waggled her eyebrows at him. Or tried.

"You sent me romance novels," he growled.

She plucked a book off the top of the stack in her
arms and waved it at him. The pages bristled with Post-
it notes. "I sure did, but you're the one who read them.
I didn't force you to do that."

"I was curious. I marked a few ideas to try out." He
advanced on her until her back was pressed against the
wall and his forehead rested against hers, the books
trapped between them.

"Were you planning on tying me up?" She sounded…
curious.

Now that she mentioned it? Yeah. He was.

"I interrupted your shower."

She blinked, confused by his change of topic. "The
water heater's temperamental. It takes a while for the
water to heat up. I was waiting it out."

He could imagine a dozen different ways to fill the time. "It would be a shame to waste water."

A grin curved her mouth. "You bet."

She slipped out of his hold, setting the books down on the floor before heading for the bathroom down the hall. Following her was no hardship at all because her soft cotton shorts hugged her butt, the skimpy fabric riding up with each step she took. Bare legs, bare feet. He couldn't wait to bare her completely.

When she reached the bathroom door and opened it, steam billowed out, so the heat must have finally kicked in. He stepped in behind her, closing the door and shutting them both into a hazy cocoon.

"I'm only asking one question tonight."

"Ask away." She bent over and pulled a stack of towels off a shelf.

"Do you trust me?"

THE FUNNY THING WAS, Mia did. With her body, at least. The stuff going on in her head was all hers. He turned her on—and he made her laugh. She'd never expected to find both sex and friendship in the same sexy, Tag-shaped package.

"Yes." She dropped a towel into his hands. "I do."

"Good," he said.

"Do I need a safe word? Are we having kinky sex?" She'd have to choose her books very carefully next time.

His finger pressing against her lips had to be the sexiest turn-on ever. "Shhhh. Trust me to make this good for you. Let me give you what you need tonight."

There was that word again. *Need.*

"I'm leaving soon," he said huskily, his thumb caressing her cheek. "I know you don't want a real guy in your life right now. I'm the practice guy."

He knew a whole lot of things, probably more than she did. Funny how *trust* felt like a much bigger word than five letters—and like exactly the right word to describe her feelings for Tag. How had her practice fling become so much more, so quickly?

His jeans did nothing to hide his erection. The thick, solid length of him was reassuringly familiar. She loved how she felt around him. Not just sexy and aroused—although she definitely appreciated those feelings—but safe. Desired. *Wanted.* She grabbed his butt, pulling him closer.

"If you came over here to have sex, let's get started already."

"We're doing this my way." He reached over and turned off the water. The steam filling the bathroom softened the rugged angles of his face, covering everything with a white haze. "And I'm taking you against the countertop."

"Here?" Her bathroom wasn't large, containing a shower, a vanity and a large wall-mounted mirror. It was a perfectly ordinary counter, too, with all her things lined up in a neat row. Toothbrush. Dental floss. Mouthwash. On the sexy scale, her bathroom ranked somewhere between a one and a two.

"Now." His hand pressed against the small of her back, guiding her forward. Okay, she'd play.

"Turn around. Bend over."

When she hesitated, he eased her legs apart. Not roughly, but reminding her he was in charge now. Because she'd agreed to trust him and to play this game with him. The marble countertop was slick and cool beneath her fingertips, but the smooth surface gave her nowhere to hold, so she flattened her palms against the marble and waited.

He didn't disappoint. He set a condom on the counter and stepped up behind her. The rasp of denim against her bare thighs was followed by the hardness of his thighs as he shoved his jeans and his boxers down. He ran his fingers down her spine, tracing the dimpled indentation above her butt, and she shivered. God, if he got her this worked up from such a simple touch, what would happen when he touched her elsewhere?

"Trust me." Another command. *Okay.*

He kissed her neck, her ear, and the whole time his hands covered hers, holding hers in place. She could get free in a heartbeat, but his fingers threaded through hers were a reminder. She'd agreed he was in charge. She'd let him take control of her body, but she wanted fast, not slow.

"Tag—"

"I'm going to make sure you get exactly what you need."

Please.

He transferred her left hand to his right, braceleting her wrists with one hand. With his other, he worked her shorts down, leaving her in just her tank top and panties.

"Pretty." He ran a finger down the back of her panties until he circled her entrance. "But not as gorgeous as you."

She groaned. "You talk too much."

"And you need to learn to take your time." Gently, he slid her panties down her thighs. "These are too lovely to ruin. I'd like to see you in them again."

He pressed small kisses against her shoulder and

down her spine as he worked her tank top up. Her bare, heated skin brushed the slick marble and she hissed.

"No bra. I like it."

She liked it, too. She arched back against him, trying to capture his erection between her thighs.

"Nuh-uh. I'm not done playing with these."

He thumbed her nipples as if he had all the time in the world, and she shuddered. His warm palms cupped the soft, tender swells, while his mouth explored her ear. "You remember our deal?"

"You're going to have to remind me."

She bumped against his erection again, hoping to hurry him up some.

"I'm setting the pace tonight. You're taking orders, Sergeant."

"Well, you might want to consider picking up the pace some, sailor, because parts of me are plotting mutiny."

Her suggestion might have sounded better if she hadn't gasped at the end. He leaned in closer, his dog tags brushing against the sensitive skin of her throat.

"Wider." His leg pressing against her wet core made his next order shockingly clear. There was no hiding the sounds of wetness, because she was slick and needy for him.

He fingered her opening, spreading her juices around and then pushing inside.

"That feels so good."

Oh, yeah. She gasped out something, and he added a second finger, pumping himself slowly in and out.

"More." She needed more. His fingers weren't enough.

"Greedy." He nipped her ear lightly, and she bucked

against him, taking him deeper. His thumb swept across
her clit, and this touch felt even better, good enough to
make her moan. He liked it just fine, too, because his
erection was iron hard, rubbing against her butt, and the
steam in her bathroom sure wasn't all from her shower.

She could feel the spasms building low and deep, her
clit starting to throb beneath his thumb. She pushed her
fingers into the hard marble. She couldn't touch him—
or herself. Her skin was damp, her core tightening as
he drove her closer to the edge.

He was *killing* her. "Now."

And he was feeling merciless, because he chuckled,
the raspy sound shooting straight to her core. "Mia,
sweetheart, I make the rules tonight."

MIA WASN'T A small woman, thank God, but his big
hands nearly swallowed up her hips as he held her in
place for his first thrust. Her skin was soft, her hip
bones a tempting line he traced beneath his fingertips.
Fast or slow—he didn't know what he wanted, just that
he wanted it all. With *her*.

She canted her butt out, the smooth globes brushing his erection. Oh, she knew what she did to him.
She might have agreed to let him be in charge, but no
way he was in control. Yeah, he lost it for this woman
every time, and they both knew it. His cock ached for
her, and his hands trembled as he tore open the condom
and smoothed the latex down.

She looked over her shoulder at him. "Come back."

He tapped her butt with his palm, enjoying her small
outraged hiss. Her butt flexed, but she didn't let go of
the counter and she didn't move. "Someone needs to
learn to ask nicely."

"We'll work on that another night," she gritted out. "Otherwise, I might have to kill you."

He pressed against her opening. She was slick and wet, pure heaven fisting him, first one sweet inch. Then two.

"Is this payback for the paint?" Her question was more moan than complaint.

He grimaced against her throat. "This is me slowing us down."

Bracing himself on either side of her, he teased her with just the tip of his penis, loving how her folds parted around him, her body trying to take him deep inside. She rubbed herself against him, and suddenly going slow was a whole lot less attractive.

"Fuck." He needed to make this perfect for her.

"Yes. Now." She groaned, arching back, a woman on a mission.

"Watch me." He tapped the mirror in front of them, clearing away the steamy fog. Her cheeks were flushed, her lips parted. When her eyes met his, he thrust slowly. Stopping when her eyelashes fluttered closed was pure torture.

"Open your eyes, sweetheart. Watch us."

Her eyes snapped open and she groaned again. "Now you're just being mean."

He fisted her ponytail. "Your hair drives me crazy." He wrapped the long strands around his hand. With his other hand, he gripped her hips. Not hard enough to bruise, but hard enough to anchor her as he pushed slowly inside.

She pushed back against him, taking him deep. "Faster."

"Slower," he commanded.

She squeezed him deep inside her, but she was at his mercy. Wide open. And they were both loving every minute of it. He could feel her coming, her body clinging to his. She climaxed, and her pleasure pushed him over his own edge. Not holding back, he thrust deep. His hips slammed into hers, skin slapping against skin in a sweet unmistakable bark of sound as he spiraled out of control. His harsh breathing filled the bathroom, and, damn, now he was the one not looking in the mirror, because he'd never felt like this before.

She slowly pulled her hands away from the countertop. "Let me go?"

Absolutely. He really, really needed to let her go, before he got so used to holding her that he couldn't not. And he would—just as soon as his legs would hold him. He'd spent a lifetime catching people who were in one kind of a free-fall or another and then letting them go once they were back on their feet. He was good at the rescue, but he sucked at the next part. When the chopper landed, he handed over his rescue in the basket and moved on. He wasn't the EMT or the doctor. His part was important, but it was really only the start of something bigger. And he'd never stuck around to see what *something bigger* might entail. Starting now couldn't be part of his plans.

He dropped a kiss against her throat and then he let go.

See? Easy as hell.

15

Mia headed down to Pleasure Pier for a simple beer after work. She'd been invited by her not-quite-fiancé on a double date with Piper and Cal. Both the beer and the date were perfectly normal activities, she reminded herself. She wanted *normal* in her life, and that meant getting out there and doing things like this.

Nevertheless, her feet slowed to a crawl as soon as she reached the start of the pier. There were too many people, too close. Which was silly. She needed to get over this. Now and not some indefinite day in the future. Tag was waiting for her at the pier's far end, which should have been motivation enough. He'd looked particularly hot and kissable at work earlier, and she had definite plans to get her hands on him.

More than a few people greeted her as she power-walked her way down the pier toward the swing carousel. She nodded and smiled, but kept on going. If she stopped, she might not start again. It was nice, though, feeling like she belonged here a little. People knew her name and her face. When she reached the carousel, Piper was shrieking as she rode past, Cal by her side.

It was downright cute, the way he stole a kiss when the swings arced out over the ocean, Piper's brown hair flying around them, her hands grabbing Cal's shoulders and hauling him close.

Maybe Tag would be up for a ride, and she'd have the perfect excuse to get handsy with him, too. She would have suggested it, except she could imagine how that would end—not with erotic hanky-panky, but with motion sickness–induced nausea. *Really sexy.* Plus, right now she needed just a moment of peace and quiet.

Before Cal and Piper could spot her, she stepped into the shadows lining the far side of the pier. An almost painful awareness hummed through her body, as if she'd touched a live wire and invited ten-thousand volts of electricity to course through her veins. Kids screamed and it was happy noise, she reminded herself. *Good.* She'd make it her self-appointed mission to retrace her steps to the end of the pier, buy a beer, and then fall back. Three hundred yards. One thousand steps. She could manage that.

A pop and a sharp noise on her six.

Flash bang.

No.

Sand rippled in front of the Humvee and exploded in front of the windshield in a wild, shifting column as the too-quiet *pop-pop-pop* of machine-gun fire filled the air, and something underneath the vehicle exploded, driving the front half of the Humvee up. Win rock-paper-scissors and ride shotgun—and live. Sit in the backseat and die. They'd laughed as they played for their lives.

And she'd won. She'd gotten out. She'd come home. Or most of the way. She'd worried she wouldn't know what to do with herself stateside, that maybe she couldn't shake her training or the traumatic memories.

Home. She forced her eyes open, drinking in the boards of the pier and the distant slap of the waves. *Not the desert.* She was crouched on the ground, back to the railing, because that way no one could come up behind her. And yet she must have been completely out of it, because strong arms wrapped around her, anchoring her to the present, and she hadn't heard him coming.

"Sergeant. Mia. Snap out of it." The rough-tender tone of Tag's familiar voice rumbled in her ear made her name sound so much like *mine.* "Just a kid with a balloon," he whispered hoarsely.

"Evac," she ordered. It was always better to be safe than sorry.

She felt rather than saw his nod as Tag scooped her up in his arms and started sprinting. Going somewhere, anywhere. She didn't care as long as that somewhere had plenty of space. *Quiet.* And Tag.

Home.

TAG'S HEART POUNDED and not because he'd sprinted the length of the pier with Mia in his arms. He exhaled raggedly, carrying her down the steps onto the beach. Jesus. He'd almost had heart failure when she'd dropped to the ground, lost in her own world. He couldn't fight invisible ghosts, couldn't stand between her and the nightmares in her head.

Which, by the way, would only invite a verbal butt-kicking from her because Mia had made it perfectly clear she neither wanted nor needed rescuing. She'd tell him she had this, which made her the sweetest, prickliest liar he'd ever kissed or held.

"Hey," he said, looking down at her as he crunched across the sand, because he was positively on fire in the conversation department. She ignored him, sucking air in like a dying woman. Between each breath, she counted. *Onetwothree.* The numbers ran together in a mumbled litany and didn't seem to be doing the trick, because her fingers twisted the back of his T-shirt.

He tried again.

"I realize you like to do things by yourself, but I'm hoping you can make an exception tonight." He laid in a course for the older pier, the one locals used for fishing. Unlike Pleasure Pier, which was lit up like a Christmas tree, the old pier was dark and silent. He figured she'd like that.

She nodded, more than a little desperately, so he took that as permission to proceed with his rescue mission. He took them beneath the pier where it was dark and shadowy in the best kind of way, cutting out the light and noise from the Pleasure Pier.

She unburied her face from his shoulder and looked up at him. "Just so you know, I'm seriously considering becoming a hermit."

He knew she saw the small smile that touched his mouth, and not just because she halfheartedly dug her elbow into his side. This close, she couldn't miss a thing. There wasn't any space left between them. No distance. He had a feeling it wasn't just a matter of inches anymore. Nope. He was falling for Mia, and it could only end badly.

"Discovery Island's short on everything but sea caves. The accommodations would be wet."

Her lashes fluttered. "I can handle a little water."

He'd bet she could. His knees felt a little wobbly

just remembering the terrified expression on her face, though, so he sat down on the sand, cradling her on his lap while he reached for his boots. She wriggled, but he pinned her in place with one arm, working on his laces with the other.

"Just not people."

A muscle ticked in his jaw. "Sometimes they drive me crazy."

"Yeah." She settled in against him, so he slid his hand up to rub the back of her neck. Her hair clung to his fingers, smelling like coconut shampoo. She'd left a bottle behind in his shower and he might have used it himself. Once. Or twice. "You want to talk about it?"

"Not in a million years," she said, which just made him more determined to hear her story.

"I think you should tell me." He kneaded the back of her neck gently. "And I'm willing to wait ten minutes, not a million years."

"You've heard war stories," she prevaricated. "I've got nothing new to add."

"I haven't heard *your* story," he said. "Although I can guess. I've had missions head south. I've lost guys."

He figured she heard the unspoken *too* because she nodded her head. He'd never seen her this vulnerable or open, like the flashback had wiped out all of her defenses. She was good at closing off her emotions and keeping her reactions hidden, even when they were having sex and she was coming. He was no open book, but no matter what the circumstance, Mia always kept a little distance between her and others. Sometimes, it was just more obvious, like right now when they were beneath the old pier, two hundred yards of sand between them and the Pleasure Pier.

"I'd like to hear *your* story," he said again.

"Okay. Have it your way," she huffed impatiently, clearly feeling better. She fingered the edge of his T-shirt, stalling for time, and he was, actually holding his breath, hoping she'd open up to him. Because, just possibly, he had *feelings* for her. It was an astonishing truth. Especially because when he thought about it a little bit more, sitting underneath the old pier and holding her in his arms, he did have a name for those feelings.

He loved her.

That scared the hell out of him. Still, he didn't have to tell her. They had plenty of secrets, so if he had one more, that was okay, and not just because she was vulnerable and trusting him to keep her safe. He'd do that. It went without saying. But this was *Mia*.

Then she looked up at him, eyes angry and scared, and he lost a little bit of his heart all over again.

MIA WASN'T ENTIRELY clear on how she'd ended up where she was. The sitting on Tag's lap part was good, but she wasn't happy the details of the journey from the Pleasure Pier to their current refuge were fuzzy. Or, more accurately, nonexistent. She'd checked out.

"I hate this," she said. "Being broken. Freaking out over a popped balloon. I handled incoming fire, and now I can't handle a kid's toy?"

Tag was smart enough to ignore the rhetorical question.

"Sucks." He rubbed her back, his big hands warm through her thin shirt. She'd picked out a pretty, loose tank with little blue ribbons for straps for their date. She might have had a fantasy—or six—about Tag undoing those ribbons. She had a new bra, too, a black lace number pushing her girls up. She'd wanted them to have a good night together, a *normal* night double dating with Piper and Cal. Instead, they were sitting underneath a pier.

"You don't want to hear it."

"I think I do."

It hadn't been her fault, and there was nothing she could have done. She wasn't omniscient. Was, in fact, damn good at her job, but the insurgent had concealed the IED in the middle of the road—where *anyone*, not just GI Jane and her team, could have driven over it—and…boom.

She hadn't even been the driver. That had been Dylan. She'd been riding shotgun with J.T. and Frankie in the backseat. One minute, they'd been bumping down the highway, and, in the next moment, the IED detonated in an all-too-familiar roar of sound. The whole world spun as dirt exploded upward, small stones falling in a pitter-patter-like rain in the summer as the blast ripped the Hummer apart. Metal and other parts—parts she wasn't thinking about *ever*—crashed down, smoke and dust rolling away in a cloud of brown. Usually, she saw the telltale column from down the road. Usually, she was the one running to pick up the pieces. Not that day.

Her ears had rung in a world gone strangely silent. Later she'd learned the IED they'd driven over had been a shoddy piece of crap and had detonated a second too late to take out the entire Humvee. Instead, when it had gone off, it had caught the rear end of the Humvee.

"We weren't even on a mission. We were headed back to base and some R & R. The guys were in a good mood.

We'd be shipping stateside in another two months, and we were almost done."

"You were ready to go home."

Base had been home of sorts, but she'd been ready for a change.

"We did our job and we did it well. If we were needed, we'd have stayed. You know how it goes."

The waves rushed in by their feet and then retreated. Other than the occasional voice passing by, they were alone. Most of Discovery Island seemed to be on the Pleasure Pier. The newer pier ran parallel to this older, smaller one. During the daytime, it attracted fishermen. After dark, however, it belonged to the lovers. At least they were quiet. No one overhead was having wild wall-banger sex. Just the occasional murmur of voices and then the longer pauses. Somewhere above them, people were kissing. Touching. She wanted the same kind of contact.

"Mia."

She was greedy. Being alive should have been enough. Instead, she shifted and swung herself over his lap to face him. He was leaning back against one of the pier posts, his legs stretched out in front of him letting the beach get his jeans wet and sandy. There was concern in his dark hazel eyes and—affection. Unfortunately, she had a bad feeling that wouldn't be enough for her when he headed back to San Diego.

"There were four of us in the Hummer. We drove straight over an IED."

"How many of you got out?" He went straight to the heart of the matter.

She could see each one of the guys who'd ridden in the Humvee with her. Frankie, who was six foot two with a head of strawberry-blond hair and a perpetual sunburn on the bridge of his nose. J.T., who hated his given names so much he only answered to his initials and spent hours coming up with nicknames for every man in his unit. And Dylan, who'd sung cartoon jingles in a booming bass voice, because no mission was complete without an earworm.

"Two and a half."

"That's—" He shook his head, unable to come up with a suitable adjective. It didn't matter. She'd heard them all, and none of them described her feelings.

"Yeah. Dylan and I were in the front, so we both went airborne, which was a blessing in disguise. We had road rash, and I didn't hear anything for three days, but pop a few Band-Aids on us and we were ready to go back out. J.T. and Frankie were in the backseat, however, and they took a direct hit."

"I'm damned sorry," he said in a low, rough voice.

"Me, too."

He kissed her then, a sweet, quick brush of his lips over hers. It wasn't enough. His mouth kissed the corner of hers. Kissed more of her. He was holding back, as if he wasn't sure what she wanted, but he'd give it to her if he could. She could feel his chest rising and falling beneath her palm, strong and certain in the darkness. No, she definitely needed more.

"We could—" She waved at the sand around them. Really, it was almost dark enough. If they moved up toward those rocks, they'd have enough cover in case someone got curious and peeked underneath the pier. And neither of them had to get totally naked. Having Tag inside her right this instant seemed like a good idea. Maybe then she wouldn't feel so cold.

"You want to get me arrested for indecent exposure?"

He didn't sound like he minded, but he stood up and carefully set her on her feet before swiping at the sand on her knees. She was pretty sure she didn't have sand on her butt, but he brushed her off there, too.

"Chicken," she accused.

"I have it on good authority sand chafes," he said, a smile in his voice.

She made a turn-around gesture with her fingers, and he obliged. Sand covered his butt. Lucky her.

"I don't want to know how you know that," she retorted, brushing a hand over his sandy bits.

"Cal has sisters," he said apologetically, making a face. "They talk. I didn't ask for details, but they volunteered. My vote is for a bed." He held out a hand. "You coming?"

She punched him lightly in the shoulder. "That has to be the worst double entendre I've heard today."

"I meant it." He stared back at her, rock solid and steady. Except he wouldn't be there always, not for her. He was headed back to San Diego, while she was staying here. She needed to savor every second with him while she could.

She slid her hand into his.

"Well, in that case, count me in."

16

"SAM BLACK. RESCUE SWIMMER." The man leaning against the front counter wore a grin and not much else. His swim trunks hung decadently low on lean hips, and he hadn't bothered with a shirt. The man was seriously cut. While Cal had warned her the new guy was putting in an appearance today, he'd failed to give her a heads-up about how attractive the new addition was.

"Mia Brandt. Office manager who's going to manage your ass."

His smile got wider. "Give it your best shot."

She did a quick hand check. No rings. The lack of jewelry wasn't necessarily conclusive, because some guys shucked their bands before they dove, but he also didn't have tan lines on his fingers.

"The guys said I could pick up a dive-shop T-shirt and a gear bag."

She eyeballed him for size—damn, did the military ever grow them small?—and tossed an extra-large in his direction.

"Got it in one." His eyes twinkled at her, not taking himself seriously. She liked that, too. Sam Black was fun.

"Welcome to the team." She thumped a stack of paperwork down in front of him. "Grab a pen and start signing."

"Maybe we should get to know each other first." He waved a paper bag of tacos from a nearby food truck. "I brought lunch."

What wasn't there to like about a guy bringing food? Free tacos were free tacos—and the company wasn't bad. Of course, he wasn't waiting for an invitation, either. He padded around the counter and joined her on the business side of things. Hooking a chair with his foot, he dropped into it and stared at her.

"Free food will not get you out of the paperwork gig," she advised him.

He nodded solemnly. "And there it is—my secret plan revealed. I'll have to come up with another one."

He caught her hand in his, running a thumb over her QVC engagement ring. Given how big and bling-y it was, he would have had to be blind not to notice it. "Nice sparkler. Off the market? Or just investing two month's salary in diamond futures?"

She couldn't possibly explain her fake engagement to Sam. However, she wasn't sure she could work up a suitably mysterious smile, either, or pretend there was nothing going on between her and Tag. Because there was something, even if it was just hot sex.

"It's complicated," she hedged.

"It always is." He let go of her hand with a mock sigh. "But if you need to uncomplicate matters, I'm here to help. Or to fetch tacos. I take direction well, and I'm an excellent team player."

His heated gaze made it clear that *team player* was some sort of pickup line. She smiled back at him. Two-legged Sam was clearly attracted to her and had every intention of making his interest known. Too bad she looked at him and just wanted to pat him on the head like her cat.

Ever since Tag had carried her off the pier like some kind of movie hero—she had Scarlett O'Hara fantasies playing in her head—she'd known two things. First, she didn't need rescuing by anyone...but if Tag wanted to play Rhett Butler to her Scarlett, she was willing to let him. Second, Tag was sexy as hell, and she loved the wicked secrets of their nights together, but...she also wanted more than hot sex from him.

In fact, when she thought about Tag, the words *for keeps* popped into her head with distressing regularity. He was part of her island fantasy, but her feelings for him ran so much deeper than that, and there was a good chance she loved him. All of which meant Sam was wasting his time. She'd take his tacos, but she wouldn't date him.

So she fixed what she hoped was a professional smile on her face. "Are you a loaner or are you here for good on the island?"

He grinned back at her. He had a nice smile, one that reached his eyes and crinkled up the corners with happy lines. This was the kind of guy she should want to be The One for her. Especially when he moved closer, his shoulder bumping hers as he emptied the contents of the bag onto her desk. She tried not to wince at the mess. Free lunch was always great, but if he got taco drippings on her paperwork, they'd be having a much less amicable conversation.

"I could be talked into staying." He divided the tinfoil-wrapped tacos into two even-Steven piles.

See? He smelled good *and* he shared. She'd bet he was a generous lover, as well.

Her pulse refused to speed up.

Damn it. She was trying here, and Sam was clearly a natural-born flirt. Of course, Sam-the-kitten was completely won over by the gift of tacos and pounced on her desk.

"Off-limits, Sam." She'd made the mistake of feeding the kitten taco meat once. Her kitten apparently had a sensitive digestive system, and they'd both paid a hefty price for that little mishap.

"It's a sign," big Sam said in a low, gravelly voice. "You named your cat after me."

They both looked at the animal, who was now trying to simultaneously chase his tail and lick his balls. His appointment with the Discovery Island vet wasn't until next week.

"I'm not sure that's a recommendation," she said wryly. She was also fairly certain that Tag had named the kitten after a Dr. Seuss character, perhaps because of its penchant to run around eating anything it saw.

"And you're different than I expected." The grin Sam gave her was crooked and more than a little sexy. Unfortunately, he also wasn't Tag. As much as she wished otherwise, the rescue swimmers weren't interchangeable, and she couldn't swap one out for the other like she would a light bulb or a spark plug.

"How so?" She leaned over, waggling a pencil for the kitten to attack.

"Sergeant Dominatrix," he said, with a shrug.

Wow. And here she thought she'd left that particular nickname behind in San Diego.

"How did you hear that one?"

He looked apologetic. "I was part of Tag's unit, so I was there when he came up with it. I shouldn't have repeated it."

If Sam called her *ma'am*, she'd have to kill him. And then the rest of his words sunk in. "Tag came up with the name?"

Sergeant Dominatrix wasn't the kind of nickname any female officer needed to deal with. She'd fought hard, trained harder. She was as good—and usually better—than any man in her division. And Tag had turned her into a punch line.

"Shoot." Sam's gaze darted toward her. "I thought you knew. After seeing the two of you together, I assumed it was—"

"A lover's nickname? A pet name?"

Wisely, Sam shut up.

She wasn't done with him yet. "Just to be perfectly clear, *Tag* is the guy who dubbed me Sergeant Dominatrix?"

"It was a long time ago," Sam offered weakly.

Not long enough. She'd naively thought she'd been making some much-needed changes to her life by staying on Discovery Island. Choosing Tag—even if they only had a limited time together—had been a departure from the orderly script of her life. He'd been a risk and a heck of a lot of fun. Someone special, or so she'd thought. Since she'd no longer been an officer, she'd been free to choose him…and she hadn't had to be anyone other than herself.

She'd worried about having a future with Tag, but apparently she should have worried about their past.

Sam stared at her, and there was no missing the look of masculine panic on his face. Yeah. He'd screwed up, and they both knew it. "I shouldn't have mentioned it."

True.

But, since that horse was out of the barn, she wasn't going to worry about Sam's regrets or his futile attempts at damage control. Instead, she was going to do *exactly* what she wanted to do.

She stood up and headed for the door. Ten minutes later, she was standing at the end of the Pleasure Pier. The water here was rougher, the waves hitting hard against the piers and the surrounding rocks. The words coming to mind were *churned up*, *wild*, and—thanks to the choppy water where the incoming water broke— *unexpected current*. This was no postcard-perfect slice of beach, and swimming here would likely be lethal.

Absolutely perfect for what she had in mind.

MIA HUNG OVER the edge of the pier glaring at the water. The last time she'd been out on the pier, she'd panicked. She didn't look spooked, but Tag wouldn't risk her safety. After he'd seen her tear out here like her hair was on fire, following was a no-brainer.

The closer he got, however, the less sure he was that this was a flashback. "Are you okay?"

In fact, if looks could kill, he'd be a dead man. "I'd say so," she bit out.

"Tell me."

Whatever it was, he'd fix it. She gave him a disgusted look, clearly marshaling her words. Sam jogged up behind him. "Sorry, man. I put my foot in it."

Great. So whatever it was, it involved wonder boy. He bit back a curse. The assessment wasn't fair to Sam. He was a good man, a good soldier. It certainly wasn't his fault Tag hated the way Mia looked at him, as if she was wondering if Sam might be a keeper.

He leaned against the rail next to her.

"Is Sam spilling secrets?" Best to know what he was up against.

She turned and glared at him. The look in her eyes was part hurt, part anger, part despair. Shit. What had Sam said? Tag's glare had Sam retreating back to the dive shop.

"Tell me you did *not* give me the nickname Sergeant Dominatrix. Because that's the one thing I'd really like to be hearing right now."

Busted.

"It was a long time ago, Mia—" Excuses. He didn't make or take them. Except apparently he did.

She shook her head. "Yes or no. Let's get this clear right now."

"I did."

Her shoulders tightened visibly. He lifted a hand, dropped it. He probably wasn't entitled to touch her right now—or ever again for that matter. He should have come clean with her, although, really, when had the moment been right to say "The nickname you hate so much? I gave it to you?"

She went right on the offensive. "I thought better of you. Instead, you made me into the punch line for a bad sex joke."

Again, true. What he'd done made him feel like a jerk. He'd tossed off a one-liner, and, worse, he'd done it because his one night with Mia had meant more than he'd wanted to accept.

"I did."

"As a penis-toting member of the armed services, you can have no idea how hard it is to be a female officer sometimes. The last thing I want my men to be thinking about when they look at me is sex. How I like it. What I look like doing it." She sucked in a breath and her hands flew to her hips. "And, news flash? Just because I know what I like and I tell you? That doesn't make me some kind of BDSM expert. It means I have good communication skills, and you suck in bed."

Hell. He wanted to wrap his arms around her and promise her it would never happen again. And it wouldn't because, quite frankly, she wouldn't be giving him the time of day, let alone allowing him back into her bed. Which was his loss, as she'd so eloquently pointed out.

"I wanted to make it up to you," he said. "I tried, okay?"

Mia spared him a glance, and the look on her face wasn't happy. *Danger.* She pushed the words out through gritted teeth. "Exactly how did you try to *make it up to me*?"

There was no good answer to her question. Wisely, he kept silent. Plus, she clearly wasn't done talking.

"Would that be rescuing me on the beach? Giving me a job? Or—" she tapped her chin with her finger— "the pity sex? Because answers two and three are definitely not my favorites, and you might want to rethink your pay-it-back approach. FYI, it definitely helps if the person you owe knows she's having makeup sex."

"I should have said something."

"Damn right."

"And I'm saying something now."

She shook her head. "This isn't middle school where you get partial credit for late homework. I'm giving you a pass on the beach thing, but you're on the hook for everything else."

"Mia—" *Let's start over? I didn't mean it?* He had no idea what to say.

"Right." She stared at him for a moment, but his brain was on empty, and he didn't have any words to give. They both knew what he should have done—and he hadn't done it. He had no one to blame but himself.

Apparently coming to the same conclusion, she tugged at his ring on her finger, and he held his hand out. She looked down at his empty hand, then flicked her gaze back up to his face. "You know what? I don't think so."

She wound up and hurled the ring over the bay. She had a good arm. The ring hit the riptide dead on and sank.

TAG HALF SHOVED OFF the side of the pier, as if he was seriously considering going in after his ring. The reaction seemed a tad excessive for cubic zirconia, but maybe it was the principle of the thing.

"Shit," he bit out. "That was a ten-thousand dollar ring."

Oops. "You bought me a real ring?"

He closed his eyes briefly. "I did."

How deep was the water here? Ripples where the ring had gone in slowly faded. Not so much as an X marked the spot where she'd chucked the band. Yeah. Story of her life. She had the real thing, and she threw it away.

"Buying real jewelry wasn't part of our deal, Tag. A fake engagement means fake diamonds. Why would you go and buy the real thing?"

He looked at her. "Does it matter? The ring is fish food."

Did it matter? Yeah, probably. But not because she was worried about throwing the equivalent of several months salary into the ocean. He'd bought her a real ring. Did that mean that he…wanted a real engagement? She'd told him over and over that she didn't want the real deal. He was her practice man and not her happily-ever-after guy. But what if she'd been wrong? What if he wanted more and that was why he'd picked out diamonds just for her?

She sucked in a breath, concentrating hard on the ocean. Say it. "I think it does matter."

"It was just a ring." He shrugged. "No big deal."

He didn't say anything more and she was already out on an emotional limb. She didn't need to cut the branch off while she was sitting on it, did she? Maybe he hadn't meant anything. He was leaving the island soon and he'd never, not once, mentioned the possibility of continuing their relationship after he deployed. If he'd wanted more from her, he'd have said something.

"Don't call me Sergeant Dominatrix again," she said.

"Got it." He scanned the ocean's surface, but she could have told him that the ring hadn't magically popped up. He was out of luck in the jewelry department. "I'm sorry."

Was he apologizing for the ring? The nickname? Both sucked. For a few brief moments, she'd thought they'd had something. It turned out, though, that both at the Star Bar and here on Discovery Island he was simply playing games she didn't know the rules to. Trusting Tag had been a mistake. She'd let him in and he'd… let her down.

There was a lesson there that she needed to learn. She turned and started to walk away. Stopped.

"Tag?"

He shifted, but he didn't come after her and that right there was lesson number two. "What?"

"Next time, make sure you insure it," she said and left.

"YOU UP FOR some shore diving?" Tag strode into Deep Dive and stopped in front of Daeg. It was time to go all in.

"Sure. When did you have in mind?" Daeg acted like Tag hadn't just slammed into Deep Dive as though he'd spotted the four horsemen of the Apocalypse. Or they hadn't just spent eight hours flying and diving. "Count me in."

"Now." Because with every passing minute, the risk increased of the current moving the ring farther and farther offshore. "Cal?"

Cal looked up from the pile of gear he was sorting. "Group field trip?"

"Mission," he said shortly. The guys didn't ask questions, just helped him grab fresh tanks and their gear bags. He did some quick calculations. He had enough surface time, and he wasn't going too deep. Diving would be fine.

Please, God, let it be fine.

Daeg slanted him a look as they slogged across the sand toward the pier "So who are we rescuing this time?"

He'd rather jump gearless from the Blackhawk than have this conversation. "Me."

Cal folded his arms on the back of the front seat and

poked Daeg's shoulder. "He's the king of one-word answers today. What are the odds the next word is *Mia*?"

Bull's-eye.

"Got it in one," he admitted.

"I'm assuming she's not drowning or trapped on a burning vessel," Daeg drawled. "Because, if that's the case, I'm going to remind you to dial 911 first."

"Okay, smart-ass. You want me to say it? Fine." He took a breath, let it out. "We hooked up once in San Diego. She let me take her home from the Star Bar, and we spent the night together. The attraction was still there when she showed up here, and the whole damned island kept trying to set me up. She said she didn't mind pretending to be my fiancée and it just seemed like a good idea."

Daeg punched him in the shoulder. "Here's a clue, dude. When someone asks you out on a date, you should feel free to use the word *no*."

He'd had hot sex.

He'd had the best night of his life.

But they *hadn't* had a relationship. That hadn't come until Discovery Island.

"So, just for our edification, at what point did 'fake engagement' become 'real engagement with a real ring?'" Cal asked.

He didn't know. He tightened his grip on the tank, because damned if he could figure it out. He and Mia had had chemistry from the moment they met, an out-of-this-world sexy attraction for each other. He'd never felt like that for anyone else, before or since, and he got the impression she shared those particular feelings.

And then…what he'd felt had been *more*.

He was leaving in a week, and he wanted to stay.

There was nothing fake about his feelings for her. She was his. His one and only. His pain-in-the-butt, take-charge, stubbornly fantastic woman. Or she had been, and then he'd thrown it all away, as easily as she'd chucked his ring. She made him think about things he'd sworn weren't on the table for him. Things like *longer than six damn weeks* and *possibly forever.*

Okay. Definitely forever. He cared about her in ways he had no intention of explaining to Cal and Daeg, although, judging by the sympathetic looks on their faces, they already knew. Funny how the beach looked the same—albeit Mia-less—and the riptide was still alive and kicking just offshore. The rocks would make the shore entry tricky, and then they'd have to deal with the currents.

Cal eyed the water and shook his head. "I can give you a few words. Boneheaded. Stupid. Doomed to failure. Take your pick. FYI, those apply to this dive site as well as to your relationship skills."

He was all that. The thing was, when he was with Mia, he was also something more. *Someone* more. He wanted to be that man all the time.

"I'm not disagreeing, but I'm getting her back." Somehow. When he came up with a good plan, which might take the next ten or twenty years, by which time she'd definitely have moved on. Damn it.

Daeg whistled. "And this leads to us shore diving because…"

"Because she threw her ring away."

"Groveling." Daeg punched him in the shoulder. "You're going to have plenty of practice."

"We're going to have sand in our Skivvies," Cal added.

"I don't want to know." He really didn't.

Pulling on their gear, they headed down to the water's edge. With the tanks they could stay down longer and, looking at the expanse of water, they'd need every minute they could get.

"Okay. Give me an approximate idea of where Mia launched the ring?"

Tag pointed and explained. Unfortunately, she had a strong arm. The ring had to be at least fifty feet out past the end of the pier.

"Jesus Christ," Daeg grumbled. "Next time you lose a ring, try dropping it in the shallow part, okay?" Yeah. He'd do that. He pulled on his mask and waded in. Ten feet in and the waves broke chest-high already. This was a fool's errand. He wasn't finding shit out here. Cal and Daeg moved in behind him, right on his back and looking out for him.

"Shut up and dive."

17

Not surprisingly, Mia had already put her stamp on the house, like she'd done to his damned heart. Either she was going for the English cottage garden effect or she'd simply purchased every plant available at the local nursery and then shoehorned them in wherever she'd found a spare inch. In precise rows and squares. Her front yard was a happy explosion of color and scents.

He liked it.

He climbed the steps to the front door and knocked. Busting right on in was a fiancé privilege, and she'd revoked his access permit. Still, she answered the door, which was something. And then she didn't slam it in his face. Another point for him. He hoped. God. How had Cal and Daeg *done* this? Daeg's crazy-ass T-shirts suddenly made a whole lot more sense. Maybe it was some kind of secret fiancé-fiancée communication code.

He looked at her. "Can I come in?"

She stared up at him through the screen door. Her hair was pulled back in a sleek ponytail. She looked cool, collected and one hundred percent in charge. On the other hand, she was wearing his US Navy T-shirt and not much else, which left her long bare legs on display.

Ridiculously, he felt happy just seeing her, like everything would be okay because she was here.

"No." She glared at him. It was certainly hard to interpret that kind of answer positively. So much for hope springing eternal.

"I'd rather have this conversation face-to-face, but I'll bellow from the front yard if I have to." Nope. He apparently had no shame. Good to know.

She crossed her arms over her chest, and the T-shirt rode up higher. "I don't have anything to say to you."

"Yeah. But I have some things I need to say, starting with *I'm sorry.*"

"Those words are a good start."

She turned and walked away, but she didn't slam the door closed. That was as good as an invitation, so he opened the screen door and followed her. Because he didn't want to have to do a John Cusack imitation and stand in her front yard singing with a boom box. He was even worse at singing than he was at talking.

He reached and caught her flying ponytail, gently tugging her to a stop. "Can I start now?"

She didn't look back at him, but she didn't move, either. "Hair pulling is so second grade."

"Hey. I'm desperate."

"Really?" She turned and slapped her hands against his chest. She packed quite a wallop, and he took a step backward. Her T-shirt slipped down her shoulder. No bra strap—just the pale white line from her bikini. She was beautiful and flushed. "Because I think I'm okay with your desperation."

The John Cusack thing suddenly made a whole lot

more sense. The guy probably had a cheat sheet taped to the back of the boom box. Tag should have tried it.

"Can we sit down?" Because if he stalled for time, maybe he'd have an epiphany in the extra seconds.

"I own two pieces of furniture. A bed and a cat tree. Neither of those is working for me." She whirled and headed for the back door with her little announcement. He followed her, of course. He probably always would. Yeah. He'd be ninety and chasing her around the nursing home. Best-case scenario.

She pushed open the back door and gestured toward the steps. "That's the best I've got to offer."

Worked for him. He dropped down onto the topmost step, looked up—and realized *she* hadn't intended to pull up a seat with him. She stood over him, foot tapping, and clearly oblivious to their respective angles. Because, Jesus, he had a fantastic look up her—*his*—T-shirt. Her panties were some kind of silky navy blue fabric with pink lace absolutely guaranteed to drive him crazy.

"You don't want to sit?" he said a little hoarsely. "Because I really think you should."

He knew the moment she figured out the issue. Her face flushed a deeper pink, and she dropped down onto the step beside him.

"You don't get to sleep with me just because you feel sorry for me," she announced. "And we're both going to pretend you didn't just see my panties."

He couldn't quite keep the grin off his face.

"No." He leaned in a little closer, testing the waters. "I don't feel sorry for you. But your panties happen to be truly spectacular."

She elbowed him. "Keep talking."

"You needed help. There's nothing wrong with that." He lost the battle to keep his hands to himself and reached out, carefully tugging her hair free. "The thing is, I need you, too."

"We sound like a needy bunch. Maybe we should get counseling." She didn't sound like she was in a forgiving mood, but her lips were quirking up at the corners. Maybe there was hope for him after all.

The hell with trying to be elegant or smooth. He wasn't poetic, and he'd be buying greeting cards for every major holiday because he had no idea how to put his feelings into his own words. Plus, only three words really mattered.

Which meant that all he had to say was: "I love you."

BREATHE.

She counted each breath, but she sounded like an asthmatic with a two-pack-a-day habit. *One.* Tag lounged beside her, one big, warm thigh pressed against hers. So much for keeping her distance. Being more than half-naked wasn't helping her, either, because bare skin made it all too easy to remember their bedroom activities.

"I'm no prize," he warned, when she didn't say anything. Because she was *counting* and trying not to hyperventilate. Her heart thundered in her ears, and, for all she knew, an entire tank battalion was doing wheelies in her front yard. *I love you.* What did that even mean? "I owe Uncle Sam one more tour of duty, and I'll be gone for longer than I care to think about. I'm also fairly certain I don't know how to get this relationship business right, and I'm terrified I'm going to screw it up."

"Again." She blinked fiercely and her backyard

blurred. Because of rain, she thought. Not because this man was demanding her heart and—just possibly—offering his own in exchange.

"Again," he agreed solemnly. "You see, I've met this woman, and I'm hoping she'll agree to be my everything. She's bold and confident and I wouldn't change one thing about her."

"Kick-ass." She looked up at him, and, damn it, those *were* tears in her eyes. She didn't cry. She wasn't a girly girl, and she hadn't cried in years. "Don't forget kick-ass."

"Never. So, can I try again?" He held his hand out to her, his fingers closed around something.

"Okay." She extended her hand, and he dropped the *something* onto her palm. Her beautiful, gorgeous, all-too-real and sparkly engagement ring. "You found it."

He smelled like salt water and outdoors and Tag. "I'm a professional diver. And I may have enlisted the troops. Cal says to tell you that you have one hell of an arm. He'd feel better if you put it back where it belonged, on your finger."

"This is all for Cal's benefit?"

Tag plucked the ring off her palm, turned her hand over and slid the ring back on her finger. "Not really, but I'd feel better if you told me you loved me and were going to marry me. I'm flexible on the order."

She gave him a slow smile. "Oh, the choices."

"I'm hopeful, but I don't want to make any assumptions."

She swung herself onto his lap, straddling his hips so she was face-to-face, mere inches of space between them. Cupping his face in her hands, she knew she believed in second chances. "I love you."

"You do?" he asked gruffly, like he needed to hear her say it again.

"I do." He'd opened up to her, so she could do this for him. It was that trust thing again. She trusted Tag. She trusted that the two of them together could be so much more than either of them alone could be. "I like letting go with you. *For* you. You're my lifeline when things get rough. I didn't know when I landed on Discovery Island that I'd be coming home to you."

Just to prove her point, she leaned down and kissed him. He didn't seem to mind, because he kissed her back. When eventually she lifted her head, both of them were breathing hard.

"I'd like to propose a new nickname," he said.

He had a thing about putting names on things and people. She, on the other hand, just wanted to enjoy the moment. "Do you think that's wise?"

He winced. "How much worse can I do?"

True. He'd kind of already hit rock bottom in the naming department. She slid her hands around his neck and drew him closer, getting ready to kiss him again. And then maybe again, just for good measure. Two inches was too much. "Give it a shot."

"Sergeant Mine."

"That's not terribly catchy."

"No." He nuzzled her neck. "But I'm hoping it's true."

"You need a nickname."

"You wouldn't," he said.

Oh, but she absolutely would. "Senior Petty Officer Naval Air Crewman Hottie of the Year doesn't have quite the ring I was going for. Too many syllables."

"Thank God for Navy job titles." He grinned at her and slipped his hands beneath the edge of her T-shirt.

"I could just call you Mr. Brandt."

"Is that a proposal?" His eyes crinkled at the corners with the smile he couldn't hold back.

The man holding her so close was damned sexy, but the emotions flooding her were so much more. Happiness and hope. Love and lust. She had it all with this man.

"I do have a ring," she pointed out. "And you went to all that trouble to bring it back to me. It would be a shame not to use it."

"I'm always coming back," he said huskily. "You can count on me."

Nothing else mattered, because he was right. He'd be coming home to her and the rest of it they'd figure out as they went along.

"I love you," she said, pulling him into her for that next kiss and the kiss after that.

* * * * *

#843 A SEAL'S PLEASURE
Uniformly Hot!
by Tawny Weber

Tessa Monroe is used to men falling at her feet, but Gabriel Thorne is the first one to kiss his way back up to her heart. Can this SEAL's pleasure last, or will their fling end in tears?

#844 INTRIGUE ME
It's Trading Men!
by Jo Leigh

Lisa Cassidy is a PI with a past and Daniel McCabe is the sexy doc she's investigating. But everything changes after an unexpected and sizzling one-night stand...

#845 THE HOTTEST TICKET IN TOWN
The Wrong Bed
by Kimberly Van Meter

Laci McCall needs to lie low for a while so she goes home to Kentucky. She doesn't expect to end up in bed with Kane Dalton— her first love and the man who broke her heart.

#846 OUTRAGEOUSLY YOURS
by Susanna Carr

To revamp her reputation, Claire Miller pretends to have a passionate affair with notorious bachelor Jason Strong. But when their fling becomes a steamy reality, Claire can't tell what's true and what is only fantasy.

———

REQUEST YOUR FREE BOOKS!
2 FREE NOVELS PLUS 2 FREE GIFTS!

red-hot reads!

YES! Please send me 2 FREE Harlequin® Blaze™ novels and my 2 FREE gifts (gifts are worth about $10). After receiving them, if I don't wish to receive any more books, I can return the shipping statement marked "cancel." If I don't cancel, I will receive 4 brand-new novels every month and be billed just $4.74 per book in the U.S. or $4.96 per book in Canada. That's a savings of at least 14% off the cover price. It's quite a bargain. Shipping and handling is just 50¢ per book in the U.S. and 75¢ per book in Canada.* I understand that accepting the 2 free books and gifts places me under no obligation to buy anything. I can always return a shipment and cancel at any time. Even if I never buy another book, the two free books and gifts are mine to keep forever.

150/350 HDN F4WC

Name _____ (PLEASE PRINT)

Address _____ Apt. #

City _____ State/Prov. _____ Zip/Postal Code

Signature (if under 18, a parent or guardian must sign)

Mail to the **Harlequin®** Reader Service:
IN U.S.A.: P.O. Box 1867, Buffalo, NY 14240-1867
IN CANADA: P.O. Box 609, Fort Erie, Ontario L2A 5X3

Want to try two free books from another line?
Call 1-800-873-8635 or visit www.ReaderService.com.

* Terms and prices subject to change without notice. Prices do not include applicable taxes. Sales tax applicable in N.Y. Canadian residents will be charged applicable taxes. Offer not valid in Quebec. This offer is limited to one order per household. Not valid for current subscribers to Harlequin Blaze books. All orders subject to credit approval. Credit or debit balances in a customer's account(s) may be offset by any other outstanding balance owed by or to the customer. Please allow 4 to 6 weeks for delivery. Offer available while quantities last.

Your Privacy—The Harlequin® Reader Service is committed to protecting your privacy. Our Privacy Policy is available online at www.ReaderService.com or upon request from the Harlequin Reader Service.

We make a portion of our mailing list available to reputable third parties that offer products we believe may interest you. If you prefer that we not exchange your name with third parties, or if you wish to clarify or modify your communication preferences, please visit us at www.ReaderService.com/consumerschoice or write to us at Harlequin Reader Service Preference Service, P.O. Box 9062, Buffalo, NY 14269. Include your complete name and address.

HB13R2

Tessa Monroe looked at the group of men who'd just walked in.

Her heart raced and emotions spun through her, too fast to identify.

"Why is he… Are they here?" she asked her friend Livi.

"The team? You don't think Mitch would celebrate our engagement without his SEALs, do you?" Livi asked as she waved them over.

As one, the men looked their way.

But Tessa only saw one man.

Taller than the rest, his shoulders broad and tempting beneath a sport coat the same vivid black as his eyes, he managed to look perfectly elegant.

His gaze locked on her, sending a zing of desire through her body with the same intensity as it had the first time he'd looked her way months before.

Tessa Monroe, the woman who always came out on top when it came to the opposite sex, wanted to hide.

"That's so sweet of his friends to come all this way to celebrate your engagement," she said, watching Livi's fiancé stride through the crowd to greet the group.

"They're all based in Coronado now. Didn't I tell you?" Livi asked, her eyes locked on Mitch as if she could eat him up. "Romeo's the best man."

Romeo.

Tessa's smile dropped away as dread and something else curled low in her belly.

Gabriel Thorne. Aka, Romeo.

His eyes were still locked on her and Tessa could see the heat in that midnight gaze.

It was as if he could look inside her mind, deep into her soul—and see everything. All of her desires, her every need, her secret wants.

A wicked smile angled over his chiseled face, assuring her he not only saw them all, but that he was also quite sure that he could fulfill every single one. And in ways that would leave her panting, sweaty and begging for more.

There was very little Tessa didn't know about sex. She appreciated the act, reveled in the results and had long ago mastered the ins and outs of, well, in and out. She knew how to use sex, how to enjoy sex and how to avoid sex.

So if anyone had told her that she'd feel a low, needy promise of an orgasm curling tight in her belly from just a single look across a crowded room, she'd have laughed at them.

Don't miss
A SEAL'S PLEASURE by Tawny Weber,
available May 2015 wherever
Harlequin® Blaze® books and ebooks are sold.

www.Harlequin.com

THE WORLD IS BETTER WITH

Romance

Harlequin has everything from contemporary, passionate and heartwarming to suspenseful and inspirational stories.

Whatever your mood,
we have a romance just for you!

Connect with us to find your next great read,
special offers and more.

f /HarlequinBooks

🐦 @HarlequinBooks

www.HarlequinBlog.com

www.Harlequin.com/Newsletters

(H) HARLEQUIN®

A *Romance* FOR EVERY MOOD™

www.Harlequin.com